LOOKING AT THE STARS

Caroline Totton

authorHOUSE®

AuthorHouse™ UK Ltd.
500 Avebury Boulevard
Central Milton Keynes, MK9 2BE
www.authorhouse.co.uk
Phone: 08001974150

First published by AuthorHouse 07/11/2011

ISBN: 978-1-4567-7983-2 (sc)
ISBN: 978-1-4567-7984-9 (e)

Chapter 1 – Paris

I

There she was, installed in a cosy corner of the James Joyce pub in Port Maillot, Paris. The table in front of her strewn with postcards, pens, a diary, a copy of *Le Monde*, a big, half-drunk pint of Guinness, a half empty pack of Gauloise Blondes Légères and her camera. My little sister. Her eyes were twinkling with health and beer. We hugged hard. I sat down opposite her on the wooden seat and caught my breath. Here we were together at last in Paris. I bought a small French beer and sipped on it listening on and off to M's incessant chatter about living in France, her job as a language assistant at the university, her friends, her flat. Here I was after months of planning and worrying sitting in Paris sipping beer and basking in the glow of the first day of the rest of my life.

Three beers later we decided to look for accommodation for the night. I had been wondering about that since coming into the pub but the flow of lively chatter was so liquid and welcome that I sat back and pushed the mundane worries like finding a bed for the night, to the back of my mind. M was not in the slightest bit worried. As usual she was completely blasé about the whole thing.

"We needn't bother till later, let's have another drink first", she dismissed me waving her cigarette in the air.

"But remember Berlin," I began sensibly. The older wiser and ordinary sister.

"We got so drunk on snaps and Berliner Pilsner that we nearly left our bags in the pub, then by the time we found our way to the nearest affordable hotels, it was 2 a.m. we paid double what we'd expected and didn't even get a full night's sleep."

"It'll be fine, relax," she smiled, "all we have to do is get the metro to Montmartre - there are loads of cheapies there - check into the first one we see that looks reasonably clean," she shrugged, "chill, it'll work out. *Santé* to your *voyage d'aventure*", she winked and raised her pint glass.

So I relaxed, had another sip of beer and lit up another cigarette. M continued to chat about her new job and friends. She looked much the same, maybe a little thinner, a little older. She had that milk-white skin that was almost transparent, a snub nose with a smattering of pale freckles around it, a round chin and steely, grey-blue eyes. It wasn't an especially beautiful face, nor was it plain. It was framed by straight, strawberry-blond hair cut into a kind of bob which had grown out, swept back from her face and held in place with childish, green, plastic bobbles. A few strands were always loose. She wore no make-up, no perfume and no jewellery. Her eyelids looked almost lilac when she closed her eyes but apart from that the face was almost colourless. The smile, however was wicked and glittering and could be smug, evil and angelic all at once. The smile could also be manipulative.

We left the James Joyce pub very late.

II

It was one of those clean, blue, transparent days when everything was sharp and defined like a photograph. There was a clarity in the air that always comes with autumn. It was cold but clear and the market was full of bright things like pumpkins and sunflowers. Orange and yellow and cobalt blue like a Van Gogh painting. I was walking slowly taking in the sights of the Parisian market, smelling the heady aromas of market day; fish and salt and spicy oils, cumin and rich tea and earthy vegetables, cut flowers, limes and musty, rustic apples. Magical smells. But I had to get real food. I was very hungry.

Last night, we had eventually left the James Joyce pub. Five beers on an empty stomach was not the way to begin a new life, but it was the way I began mine and my body was registering its rigorous disapproval. We'd taken the metro to Montmartre which was well known for its reasonably priced hotels and, as we'd agreed, checked into the first reasonably clean hotel we could find. The latter criterion was ignored as we wearily climbed the rickety steps of the 'Hôtel' (for that was its name). The word 'hôtel' had been hand painted carelessly on a wooden sign, unembellished by lights or anything remotely appealing. A pungent odour of boiled cabbage and ancient curry powder greeted us at the reception, where an unkempt middle-aged man with an exquisite moustache grunted a *"Soixant francs"* at us, and waved a fantastically dirty hand in the direction of the stairwell. We couldn't have cared less, although I insisted on checking that the room at least had a lock on the door and a window from which we could escape in the event of any sinister happenings.

It did have a lock. I peered out the window. A few meters below was a shabby linoleum-covered roof and from there one could probably drop, unharmed onto the street. We dumped our bags and slumped onto the one bed. I looked around and grimaced.

The place was, as could be predicted from the price, a dump. The floor was covered with a cracked and filthy oilcloth which curled up at the corners, inviting the fertile imagination to envision the horrors beneath. Bare electrical wires and cracked pipes ran up the walls, along with a platoon of large ants which were marching towards the ceiling. An exhausted, enamel sink leaned precariously against one wall and *la pièce de résistance* against the wall opposite, a care-worn, foul smelling bidet, which upon closer inspection appeared to have been used by previous guests as a toilet.

"Yippee! Now we don't have to go outside to use the toilet on the landing," cried M as she peered expectantly into the bidet and wrinkled her little snub nose.

Ever the optimist, I thought. Any marginally normal person would have been horrified, but here we were thanking God for the smallest of conveniences, suffering from the great madness of the Pollyanna complex. I was about to spend my first night of freedom in Paris' grimiest bedroom and one least-conducive to a good night's sleep. But at least I could pee in the bidet and didn't have to risk life and limb out on the landing in the middle of the night with God only knows who shuffling around out there. I thought, what sort of people stay in a place like this? It would be like a scene from *The Night of the Living Dead*.

"Doesn't this remind you of George Orwell's *Down and Out in London and Paris*?" M said excitedly as she fished out her cigarettes and a bottle of Evian water.

"Yes," I replied dreamily, "when I am being interviewed about the source of inspiration for my famous and great novel, wearing a splendid kaftan and turban ensemble, I shall look back at this night and...."

"Vomit!" M interjected and we both fell back on the bed laughing. I don't know what possessed me then but, being an extremely curious sort of person, I got a sudden urge to look under the blankets.

"I wouldn't get under the covers if I were you," I said, quickly replacing the edge of the sticky blanket I'd just peeled back.

"It seems our previous occupant left a reminder of him or herself on the sheet."

M leapt over to look, not being able to resist, even though it was inevitably going to be unpleasant. There lay on the once-white sheet, a faint yellow stain and a solitary pubic hair, like a message and a signature.

Despite all this, we slept quite well. Only once was I awakened during the night. Strange music floated through the open window. Getting up to pee in the 'en-suite', I looked out into the street below and saw what looked like a circus tent. The music was coming from the tent. It was enchanting, Arabic and somehow haunting. I was at once reminded of Marseille, though I have never been there. I strained in the half-light to see into the tent as the front flap was open. The smell of incense drifted up, mixed with the filthy odours of the street, rotten vegetables and urine. Suddenly a woman came out of the tent carrying a monkey on her shoulder. She was dressed in baggy, Turkish style trousers and a sort of cape. I stared at her in the bad light and could just make out her features. She had strong handsome, exotic features but the skin was heavily lined and the eyes, melancholy diamonds, were sharp but full of sadness.

Suddenly, she turned her head sharply and looked straight up at me. Her eyes pierced me. I felt a shock as if I'd been wading in shallow tepid water and then the bottom had suddenly shelved and I was plunged, up to the neck, in to iciness. As well as the directness of her gaze, it was the way she turned her head and body to look at me. The angle was completely unnatural. She could not have looked in my direction accidentally. She had to turn her body 180 degrees as well as look up to see me. I must have made some noise. That was it. My heart started to thump and I hitched a breath and drew my head sharply in.

I wondered, at that moment, what on earth it would be like to be her. I felt as if we had somehow connected. For a millisecond we had been the only two people in the world. Two women from different planets, on the same street just looking at each other. As my heartbeat started to regain its normal rhythm I realised I had overreacted. I was spooked by being in a strange city, in the middle of the night, in the dirtiest hotel room in Paris. This woman, whoever she may have been, had probably heard me lean out of the window and looked up automatically. That was all. I settled back into bed breathing deeply to calm myself. Drifting off to sleep, I wished I would dream about her but I didn't.

The next morning, the tent was gone. I wondered if I had imagined it all or had some sort of crazy lucid dream. I still felt a little spooked, the way one does the morning after a nightmare when the memory is fresh but too fragile to stay long. I longed to get out of this dump. M was noisily enduring a hangover and begged for aspirins, tea and bread, in that order. I dressed quickly, splashed some water on my face and popped a piece of chewing gum in my mouth instead of brushing my teeth. There was no way I was going to be on anything more than a nodding acquaintance with that sink. I tried to get her out of the stinking bed to come with me and go for breakfast and coffee in some disinfected establishment where the waiters wore starched, white aprons and smelled of hair cream. But she wouldn't come.

I stopped analysing the previous night's events and, with relief, spied a tiny boulangerie on the next corner. The aspirins and tea would have to be gloriously anticipated. I bought a baguette, a pain au chocolat - to eat on the way back - and some bottled water. I was feeling much happier now. The weirdness of last night was diluted with the sunshine and the ambiance of this gorgeous city. I walked back briskly to the hotel 'Hôtel', as it modestly named itself, and ran two-at-a-time up the rickety stairs. I glanced into the reception area for an instant as I passed, only to be stared at by at least six pairs of big, curious eyes. The proprietor's family were all getting washed and dressed in the little room which served as the reception area and apparently, additionally, as the family's living area. There, behind the wire of the reception booth, sat mother and four or five sticky children in various states of undress and washing, like a family of exhibits in a zoo enclosure. I raced quickly on to the second floor. I anticipated M's grin when I produced the bread and water. She should be out of bed and dressed by now. God help her if she was still asleep. I burst in.

She wasn't there.

I looked round the room to double check but no, no-one was there. I called out and my voice sounded small and weak and dead; hardly worthy of a response. I sat down on the bed and tried to think rationally. Could she have popped out for some cigarettes? No, there lay on the bed, in a crumpled pack three or four Gauloises Blondes. What then? Probably she just got fed up waiting for her tea and bread and marched out of the fetid hotel atmosphere into the spiced Parisian air?

Her things were still there. Her battered, grey hold-all with the frayed strap and the peeling, sewn-on "Ireland" patch depicting the shamrock. Her camera in its case lay on the bed. She hadn't gone far. My initial panic was turning to irritation. It was just like M to impulsively run out like that, whilst I was off getting us breakfast. She would be back in a minute.

I would just have to wait a while, relax, smoke a cigarette and enjoy the second day of my new life in this beautiful city and the allure of impending adventure around me.

Suddenly, someone was banging on the door. I started and my adrenaline pump kicked in again. 'Oh lord, what now?' I thought. A man's voice called gruffly.

"*Vous devez partir!*"

I pictured the proprietor from the reception booth the previous night. I saw his rotten teeth, his dark pools of eyes and his flamboyant moustache. I couldn't leave right away, I thought, beginning to panic again.

"*Oui, monsieur, je comprends...nous allons maintenant.*"

I replied in the same weak, flat voice, then kicking myself for calling the rude ass 'monsieur'. Surely someone as seldom acquainted with soap as he, deserved no such title. I heard my voice, pathetic and with a bad French accent and it had no resonance, no depth. It rose briefly around the room like a leaf in a faint breeze then fell flat and dead against the stained walls. I felt like a little girl again. That little seven year old girl in a crimpoline dress made of old curtains who didn't want to go into the sweet shop because she was scared of the man with the moustache behind the counter.

I gathered up my bag and M's bags, her camera and the plastic bag of odds and ends one always manages to acquire on a trip, and walked out of the hotel. I glanced at the proprietor on the way out, trying to look menacing and failing miserably.

Mummy had sent me into the sweetshop and she was irritable and short tempered that day. She'd scorn me if I didn't go in. "All the other children go in alone, why can't you?" she'd snapped and I wanted to cry but didn't dare. So in I crept and stood at the back of the shop, where hopefully no-one could see me. The man behind the counter wouldn't see me anyway. He had these piercing, insectile eyes but they would pass over me as if I was invisible and rest on the smiling, cheeky faces of the other eager children who strained to get his attention, coins bunched up in tight little cherub fists. But he never saw me. I was standing still in the shadows and couldn't quite meet his eyes.

I thought about asking the proprietor on my way out when M had left and if she'd left a message but my courage failed along with the French sentence I was trying to form in my head. I would go to a café and drink some good coffee and formulate a plan. If all else failed I could go on to Reims alone. I had the address of the studio we were taking there. I felt better as soon as I got outside. The ghostly little girl in the sweet shop was also gone, at least temporarily.

Chapter 2 – Kristiana

I

They were seated in a dimly lit Bistro on the corner of Rue Jean d' Arc. Kristiana was giggling into her hand, her long chestnut-coloured hair spilling onto the table. She had a beautiful face, full mobile mouth and flashing, black eyes. But there was something about that mouth that was rather ugly when she held a particular expression; something cruel.

I happened upon them purely by chance when I'd given up hope of trying to find M and was wandering aimlessly through the raddled streets of Montmartre, feeling more at ease. My mood changed bit by bit as I left the realms of the rank hotel. Along with relief, I felt a queer sort of electrical jolt as I passed hastily by the man with the luxurious moustache. A shot of adrenalin; I was free. I had escaped. So had the long ago little girl with the sticking out frizzy, red-blond hair and the stick-legs, who ran out of the sweet shop and told a little white lie. Only a little lie and it set her free so it was worth it. It set her free from the hot blush which would have followed the stammered, barely-audible words as she asked for the sweets. It set her free from the inevitable feeling of shame and fright as his eyes passed over her and onto the next, more eager face.

"They didn't have any mummy," she said running out of the dark shop and back into the sunshine, bright eyed and panting slightly.

I couldn't remember exactly what they didn't have any of, it was so long ago. It was a simple child's lie told with a simple child's conviction, except it wasn't believable to an adult. Especially one who could read a child like an open book and who could see her squirming in there, even through the solid shop walls - a sort of adult super power, charged by the relentless and eternal responsibility of creating another person. She had swung me around, marched me back into that dark and foreboding corner shop and up to the counter to ask the man if I had been in and asked for the "something". I could have died, standing there, head hung in shame, a crimson blush creeping up my neck, spreading out towards my cheeks, reaching my ears and burning them. The man peered over at me and shook his head. I wanted to disappear, shrivel up like a leaf and blow away on the breeze.

Nothing more was said. I had learned my lesson.

But for now I chased away these shadows. I was elated and felt braver. M had gone out for a walk. I was worrying for nothing and was not going to spoil the first day of the rest of my life being haunted by the insecurities of my childhood whilst frantically pursuing my selfish little sister through Paris with our combined baggage in tow. I would go on to Reims alone and meet her there later.

But then I spotted them in the bistro on the corner. It glowed from the inside, all cosy and candle-lit. The smell of warm croissants drifted out onto the cold street. There, in the window at the foremost table as if they'd been sculpted there and given the title 'Young Parisians at Coffee', illuminated in the light and warmth of the café centre-piece candle like Van Gogh's *Potato Eaters*, sat M and Kristiana. I almost walked right past them when suddenly I saw M and did a double take. She waved casually as if we'd arranged to meet there. As if I hadn't rescued all her things from the hotel. As if I wasn't traipsing around Paris wondering where the hell she was. As if I hadn't had to confront the angry hotelier and his moustache with my bad French.

I marched in and dumped the bags at her feet but I was determined to keep my cool and not to show I was angry or upset. Besides, I'd almost convinced myself I didn't care, I was so glad to find her.

"Charlotte!" she cried, "I was on my way back, honest. I just popped out to find you. You were away such a long time and I was *sooo* hungry and thirsty, then, my God, what a coincidence! I bumped right into Kristiana," she gushed and sprang up to greet me with a hard hug.

So it was my fault for taking such a long time to find breakfast. I took in Kristiana and nodded.

Then I said as placidly as I could manage, "Well I wish you'd waited, we had to check out and I had to drag all the bags and everything not to mention having to deal with the pleasant Mr. Proprietor."

I immediately could have kicked myself for not being more assertive, for not creating a drama like she would have done if it had been the other way around. For putting up with this shabby treatment because I didn't want to be alone.

"I'm sorry," she said, a little uncertainty registering in her steely grey-blue eyes, "I didn't think."

I shrugged and tried a convincing smile but I was still smarting a bit so it probably looked as if I was about to burst into tears. But it was readily accepted as a sign of forgiveness by M.

"Anyway, this is my best friend Kristiana," she continued," who worked with all the *lecteurs* and *lectrices*[1] last year in Troyes. What a coincidence, I was peering out the window of 'The Ritz' to see if you were coming back with the food when suddenly I spotted her walking right past the building. I couldn't believe it, what luck" she gushed, again all sparkly and impressed with herself, her uncertain moment passed and forgotten.

I stretched out a hand to Kristiana, who returned the gesture and we half-heartedly shook hands.

"Nice to meet you," I said managing a more controlled smile this time, "Charlotte."

We looked at one another for a moment. Her dark brown-black, slightly tilted eyes met my blue-grey rounded ones. I waited for the reaction to my old-fashioned name. I was called after one of those maw-mouthed, ancient aunts who had disturbed and frightened me in their funereal crisp, white shrouds and yellowed, parchment-like skin. I used to be teased mercilessly about it at school when everyone was a modern Tracey, Elaine or Deborah but I quite liked it now. It was old but rich and classic.

Kristiana smiled widely, but the corners of her full mouth twitched as if it were being moved against its will and better judgment. Then she laughed naturally, rich and deep and I liked the sound.

"Yes M told me all about you, Charlotte. *Charlotte Sometimes.*[2] It's lovely to meet you at last," she said with a European accent I could not identify.

"She's Swiss," M went on, anticipating my curiosity. Kristiana laughed a tinkling laugh this time.

"But it's not my fault," she said tossing her long, chestnut hair back and laughing at her own little joke.

1. Language assistants
2. Title of a song by The Cure

"Let me order you a cup of coffee. How do you like it?" she asked, smiling less widely this time but very sweetly.

I sensed that, underneath her welcoming and friendly smile, Kristiana was suppressing something. I felt her assured superiority swelling up within her and breaking her veneer of congeniality like a seal swimming underwater gracefully and silently but who would undoubtedly have to come up for air eventually and give itself away.

"M's been telling me all about your little adventure," she began, whilst unselfconsciously beckoning a waiter.

I felt a flicker of anger lick my belly but quickly quashed it. I didn't want to judge her too harshly. I was always too quick to judge people, making up my mind about them on a first meeting. It was one of my faults. Then again, my first impression and subsequent judgment were usually right. If I didn't like someone almost immediately then I almost always didn't change my mind. 'Little adventure,' indeed. How dare she! This twenty-something, self-assured princess. My 'little adventure' had so far consisted of leaving my job, home and friends to take up some job somewhere in a French provincial town or possibly even elsewhere. And it was all uncertain still.

"Well I was hoping my adventure won't be so little, it's felt pretty big to me so far," I replied, feeling indignant and cross, but revealing nothing.

Again the tinkling laugh, disconnected from the dialogue. It floated across the café, light as a bubble and with as much sincerity and purpose.

M sat beaming across the table busy with a cigarette and lighter. She was oblivious to our veiled battle of wits.

"All things are relative," Kristiana replied dismissing me, uncaring and un-listening.

"*Un grand café crème,*" she called to the waiter who'd sidled up to our table with an air of being very important.

Then she waved him away as one would an annoying tramp who was asking for money. He nodded and went, unaffected by her little display.

M noticed this immediately. This was the type of behaviour she devoured and desired.

"Oh I *love* the way you deal with Parisian waiters Kris," she drooled, emphasising the word love and drawing it out so it plucked at my nerves and I tensed my jaw.

"Ach," said Kristiana, "It's the only way to deal with them. They love it. They love a bit of fire you know, they can't stand people being all humble and inferior, daring not to say a word. If one behaves like a dog one is apt to be kicked."

Or have his eyes scratched out, I thought as I caught her glance. Then she averted her eye to something beyond me through the dirty, steamed up window; something evidently much more interesting. Or maybe she was seeing nothing, only basking in the after-glow of her eloquent speech.

My coffee came and I drank it. It was strong and sweet and slightly creamy. The afternoon sunlight shone through the window showing up the dirty streaks more effectively and I let Kristiana and M babble and tried to form more of an impression of her. I half listened and half stared out the window. She was young and full of the arrogance of the young and had to have the feeling that she was impressing someone. She evidently enjoyed scattering her plagiarised opinions loudly in public places and changing them according to the latest fashionable philosophy or who was listening. I didn't really care about Kristiana and her ways with French waiters. It didn't matter. M seemed to like her anyway and who was I to choose her friends. She didn't choose mine.

"Do you speak French at all?" she asked me casually as we drained the coffees.

"Only enough to get by but I suppose I shall improve whilst working in Reims," I replied.

"Oh I do think it is so important to speak a few languages and it gives one such colour to babble in different linguistic realms," she went on.

She talked about speaking a few languages as casually as if she were talking about owning a few pairs of shoes.

"Well I do have an interest in languages and linguistics in general," I said without much interest in the conversation. Kristiana's manner was making me feel like I had a rock in my stomach.

I had the feeling that she was steering the conversation towards a point where she would triumph over other mortals like me, and perhaps like M too.

"It's my greatest passion," M chimed in, releasing me from Kristiana's cat-like attention.

"My ambition is to one day publish a book with lists of all the linguistic 'fuck-ups', I mean, mistranslations and funny grammatical errors I've heard from foreigners," M continued lighting up like a light bulb and absentmindedly flicking ash over the table in full view of the waiter who was hovering nearby waiting for the cups to empty completely. Probably so he could throw us out.

"An example?" asked Kristiana, raising her eyebrows.

M thought for a moment then began to giggle, holding her hand over her mouth as she always did as if trying to push the laughter back in.

"My German friend from Berlin", She began, "once said that her cat was ill so she was going to take him to the vegetarian," she spouted barely able to finish the sentence before erupting into spasms of giggles.

I laughed too, even though I had heard it before. Suddenly, we were all laughing together and I somehow felt then that we had become mere caricatures of ourselves. It felt as if I was an onlooker, outside my body and mind, looking in on a scene from a film or a book. I suddenly became a voyeur of myself, ourselves, viewing the cosy scene through the window, rubbing a clear spot on the glass and pressing my nose against it. Three girls drinking coffee in a Parisian bistro on a white, cold autumn day. The wind outside whipping up the copper-coloured leaves into a frenzied dance. The soft lights inside representing the protected and warm and paid for; a scene, an act. A fragment of three lives whose paths crossed one day and merged for a short time. It made me think again of the woman with the monkey. It made me think of destiny.

Kristiana suddenly leapt up and looked at her watch.

"Damn I'll miss my class at Sorbonne.......no maybe if I run all the way. I have to go I have a photography class at three," she cried.

She gathered her bag and cigarettes, tossed her hair back, grabbed her coat and kissed M three times on the cheeks. Then it was my turn. She rushed against me kissing me sincerely. I smelled her hair and a faint scent of cinnamon and dust from her scarf.

"I do love your name by the way, Charlotte Sometimes, it's so cool," she said, smiling broadly.

I felt warmed by that smile and by that one simple, casual remark. Perhaps I'd been wrong about her.

"Call me M," she yelled, running out the door.

And she was gone, up the street joining the dancing, whirling leaves and the outside world.

II

On the train to Reims after a long, cold wait at the Gare de L'Est, M suddenly delved into her bag and pulled out a small thing wrapped in white tissue paper.

"Look what I found," she beamed and proceeded to un-wrap the small thing. It was a unicorn. It was a glass ornament, small and delicate with a sparkly mane and tail. It had spindly glass legs. It was pale pink and lilac and somehow greenish.

"Look," she said turning it in her small mitt, "it changes colour in the light."

Indeed it did. It was transparent then blue then opaque in the shadow. It was a lovely thing indeed. Its little fragile glass horn sparkled and its hooves were iridescent shale. It was poised with one foreleg raised, prancing and proud; a ballerina-unicorn.

"You'll break it," I said. And didn't know why I said that.

She tutted and wrapped it up again very carefully.

"Of course I won't break it, I shall put it on a high shelf and never dust it and it will bring me luck, bring us luck."

"Where on earth did you find it?" I asked, "It looks like something from the land of the *Sì*[3]"

"Oh, in wee junk shop near the Montmartre. I was poking around looking for a tabac actually and I went up this wee side street and there she was in the window. She was singing out to me. She brought me too her," M replied dreamily touching the unicorn through the tissue paper.

"May be it's a sort of talisman," I said.

"Maybe," she answered, looking peaceful and content.

---

3. *Sì* - Irish Gaelic - Folklore fairy people (pronounce shee)

Hopefully, I thought. Maybe it was a good omen, a blessing from the gods on my new life, my 'little adventure'. I reflected on the day, on Kristiana. How did I really feel about her? I tried to put it to the back of my mind and to rinse her away with the wind but something about her unsettled me. Something about her seemed odd and not quite to add up. Maybe I should talk to M about her. Then again maybe I shouldn't interfere. And I was tired. Only my second day in France and already I'd been scared by M's strange disappearance then haunted by the old ghosts of my childhood. I was in a strange country, beginning a new chapter and it was simply taking up enough energy already without worrying about my sister's friend and trying to unravel her psyche.

However I did know M inside out and Kristiana wasn't the type she usually chose as a friend. M was shrewd and merciless when it came to people who seemed insincere or who thought they were superior. Although she acted that way herself at times and there was a little hard and selfish streak in her like a skein of iron in chalk. Harder than the rest. It glinted, cold and indifferent when it surfaced and it shone like cut glass. But for the most part she was warm and caring and genuine. M didn't stand for pretentiousness or showing-off. She was too direct: "If you don't know something, say you don't know", she'd always say, "who cares if you should know? The thing is not to pretend you know because you'll look silly when you are found out and you *will* be found out."

But sometimes it was easier to pretend to know something and let it go and move onto the next thing. Admitting to being misinformed or ignorant in front of certain people could make your face sizzle and your heart pump furiously and sometimes it just wasn't worth it.

We are all vulnerable and mushy inside, I thought, as the train rocked us eastwards and northwards. Like little mobile sacks of mashed pulpy stuff. All orbiting our own planes, soft and vulnerable, turning and spinning and sometimes hitting the hard, uncaring surface and getting smashed up. It's amazing we survive at all, I continued, now amusing myself. Our soft bodies and glistening internal organs moving hopelessly in this world of granite and right angles and even more fragile, our psyches. I suppose we all need a mean streak and a veneer of something tough and if it meant pretending then maybe it was necessary for survival to do so. But we were really all as fragile as M's little glass unicorn wrapped up in tissue and cushioned between socks and t-shirts. Safely tucked away at the bottom of her bag for now and lulled, like us into a womb-like sense of security and softness; safe, but only temporarily.

When we got to Reims after the hour's train journey, I felt dog tired. My body ached, my skin itched, my eyes were grainy and I wanted to ball my fists and screw them into my eyes like a tired child. I really wanted to sleep. I wanted to be back in my own bed, in my own house listening to the wind howl and the rain beat its soothing cadence against the window, telling me how cosy and safe and dry I was and how cold and wet and unwelcoming the outside darkness was. But I wasn't going to my own bed. I was standing at a train station in a cold Northern, provincial, French town waiting for my sister to find her tobacco accoutrements and her bearings towards our new abode. We were staying at number three Rue Marie Claire Fouriérès. Two rooms above a grotty bar and parallel to the railway tracks leading in one direction to Charleville in the French Ardennes, heart of the Champagne country, and in the other to Paris. The wind was stronger here than in Paris and carried a chill from the East. It was a cruel, dry, cold, wind which flayed our skins and made our eyes water. As we trudged out of the station and towards Rue MC Fouriérès, most cafés and shops were already shut. Only a gruesome little café-tabac was open, out of which trickled a sickly green light onto the street and illuminated an old French man inside. The light inside emphasised his desiccated posture as he leaned over the bar like a lopsided scarecrow. He was like one of the dried-up leaves on the street. It felt gloomy and cheerless, dark and cold.

M drew my attention away from the old man and to some shop window displays. Therein stood skeletons and haggard witches riding broomsticks with evil and mocking faces. Bright orange Jack O'Lanterns with grinning pumpkin faces and wicked pumpkin smiles leered out at me, at us. It was almost Halloween. "Go home," they seemed to say to me, "go back, no-one wants you here, you don't belong here, you're too ordinary. Go back to your semi-detached house in your suburban area with your ordinary job and narrow-minded, insular little friends, you'll hate it here, you'll be like a fish out of water, gasping, flailing and drowning."

The ghosts of insecurity and uncertainty were back. The little girl in the sweet shop was back, she with the knocking knees and the blushing mechanism on a hair trigger. But now she was standing shivering on the edge of the sports field waiting to be chosen for a team. Waiting and waiting until the teacher at last allocated her with a sigh whilst the others laughed and teased and pushed each other around being bold, confident and fearless.

But that wasn't going to be me any more. I was thirty now, ice-cool, organised, focused, independent and slightly scornful of those who weren't. Like M. I looked up and she'd gone on ahead whilst I stared back at the witches, lost in my own thoughts for a moment.

Then I turned and ran to catch up with her big strides, her impatience getting the better of her once again.

Chapter 3 – *Samhain*[4]

T'was Halloween night and the moon was bright
Glowing, pale and round
A dozen people came to my door
But never made a sound

Ghoulish faces, witchy faces
trying out their dancing paces
In fancy dress they did impress
In red and gold and jade

But why didn't I smile when they touched my hand?
And why did I feel afraid?

I

A week later I was standing at the steam-streaked mirror in our tiny bathroom applying black eyeliner, heavily. I'd already blackened my eyebrows, applied mascara and glitter gel on my cheekbones. Blood red lipstick would complete the picture. I was going to be a witch. Only my hair disappointed me. It was dark blond and fine and silky and it curled rather than spiked. I wanted straight black thick and oily hair, witch-hair; gipsy hair. Oh why was I cursed with this unruly stuff? I needed a hat or a wig or something to disguise my fairy hair. Suddenly a reflection appeared in

---

4. *Samhain* - Irish Gaelic - Halloween (pronounce sow-in).

the mirror, a grisly white face, blackened mouth and eyes, grinning and holding a kitchen knife above her head.

"M!" I shrieked, "You scared the hell out of me and what's more I nearly put my eye out with this kohl pencil."

We both laughed. It was Halloween night and there was a fancy dress party to go to, in, appropriately, the Dark Café. M put down the knife and shoved me out of the way to peer at her make-up.

"O God, I look like some zombie horror from..some zombie horror film," she squealed, obviously delighted. Then she turned to me rather seriously.

"But Charlotte, what are you going to do with your hair?" she asked whilst back combing hers furiously with her fingers. She was evidently rather proud of the effect. It was thick and sticky with glitter and hairspray and looked fiendish. Mine did not.

I stared into the mirror then girned at myself.

"I think I'm hideous enough even with the fairy hair," I said.

M was beaming all over her face like a small, pale moon. She was excited and young. This was her evening. She had been at her new job at the local university, affectionately known as *le Fac* short for *Faculité* (faculty), for several months now. She was an English language assistant, or lectrice, and was hosting her first party for some of her colleagues and students. Later we all would go on to the fancy-dress party at the Dark Café.

This evening would be a kind of initiation, a test of popularity. Would everyone show up? What if only two or three came and we sat exchanging stilted small talk and cringing throughout long silences, nervously glancing at each other and trying to think of an excuse to leave? Or what if no-one came at all? For me, this would have been preferable to the former option. Kristiana would come, of that I was sure. Even though she'd only said 'maybe' and she had a big exhibition to put together for the end of November and she just had to work. I mused that Kristiana could hardly have any idea of the concept of work and then I was suddenly dreading meeting her again. Her tossing hair and her gleaming smiles.

M was my sister and best friend. I knew I was a little jealous of this new relationship. No-one else had the right to nudge their way into my territory, especially someone like Kristiana. Kristiana was younger than me, more beautiful, at University in Paris, studying Art; Confident. All the things I wanted to be. And here I was in France, without a job trying to be like her, trying to be M when I should be at home, married, growing slowly fat and breeding, like a milk cow.

"I think I'll have a child one day you know," M said, coyly sipping at her glass of red wine. It was as if she had just read my mind.

I turned slowly, disturbed by the intimate little sentence which had interloped our frivolous pre-party chatter. I was unsettled by its invasiveness.

"Well, where did that on come from?" I asked.

M glowed, perched on the end of the bath, long stemmed glass in hand, ghoulish make up, black shirt, black jeans, dark blue Doctor Martin boots. She looked completely the opposite of anything to do with motherhood. Motherhood equalled pastel colours, soft easy-care clothes like leggings with no hard lines or jabbing buttons to damage your delicate offspring. Motherhood equalled smiling blank serenity, pale towelling romper suits and gigantic nappy packs adorned with pictures of gurgling cherubs running on chubby legs; smiling, just-bathed angels swathed in fluffy white towels, their softly curling golden hair smelling of rosewater and sour milk.

She shrugged. "Don't know, I just sometimes have this image of me and two or three perfect blond babies, little future artists or scientists." she said dreamily.

I tutted, not knowing whether to take her seriously or not.

"You are far too young to be thinking about babies, you're not even twenty-five yet...and besides," I added wickedly, "I thought you needed a man to have a baby."

I rushed out of the bathroom and she swiped at my skirt on the way past.

"I didn't mean right at this moment," she yelled running after me into the tiny kitchenette.

"Besides that's the easy part, finding a man, let them fertilise you then dump 'em. Men don't want children anyway unless as an heir to their property or something. They only pretend to be interested in babies 'cos they think that impresses women, then they have sex and, bingo, a child. Big responsibility for the rest of your life and no escape," she rushed.

"Well that was a highly articulate outburst young M, "I laughed, "if only it were that simple."

"It is," she answered seriously, "find a good set of genes, shag him, dump him and *voila*, you have your own little heir all to your self."

"Course it would be even better if you didn't need a man at all," I added fishing around the kitchen for some matches, "then my genes would not be contaminated by some horrid man-thing's. I could reproduce myself exactly." I said beginning to enjoy this silly tirade.

M had already slumped down on the sofa and topped up her wine. I found the matches and switched off the kitchen light. Must have had a sale on at the green wallpaper shop when they decorated this place, I thought.

I continued to think about what M had said. I had never wanted children. Children were a responsibility, a liability, a big expense. Children stopped you being who you wanted to be and going where you wanted to go. Children took over your life and stopped you thinking about you. I never really knew what I wanted to do but I always knew what I didn't want. Back to the fear of ordinariness again. I didn't want the gurgling cherub on the side of the nappy pack. The Saturday morning shopping drama with sticky child in tow, the sleepless nights and days spent as a drudge. The relentless, boring child-obsessed rattle of mothers who lost their personalities along with their waistlines when they bore their offspring. They turn into track suit-wearing, pram-pushing drudges whose soul purpose in life is now being the carer and protector of the baby. I'd watched dynamic young girls with brains to burn and enough passion to change the world, one by one slowly succumb to motherhood and start to obsess about disposable versus towel nappies, breast versus bottle feeds. They'd stop talking about globalisation, climate change, the cruelty of vivisection labs. They'd become a clean slate, wiped of any opinions, except for those directly related to the child. They'd stop following current affairs, even conversations completely and become only mother. "Oh, look, he's sitting up, coughing, crying, whining, pissing, shitting, dribbling. Oh isn't he clever?" come the endless stream of moronic exclamations from mum. For she is just a nameless indefinite article now. She's 'a Mum'. No identity, except that which the child has, by existing, allowed her. She has become unaware again, blissfully, slipped back into the womb herself. The womb of simplicity, comfort, safety, routine. The womb of single focus. No need to ever think of herself again. Slightly unkempt now for baby is more important than combing her hair or washing her face. Overweight now for there is no need to be attractive now that the breeding is done and the instinct to reproduce has been fulfilled. Mum, perched on the sofa in pallid pyjamas adoringly adoring her baby.

How I hoped my sister would not turn out like that. But then that was just my somewhat perhaps twisted view. Some women and men even look forward to the prospect of parenthood. How else can you be fully excused in your self-adoration? In revering your offspring naturally you are revering and adoring yourself. An artist would be mocked and criticised for admiring his or her own creations with such vehement love but here, as a parent one can gaze at one's creation *ad infinitum*. Not only will no-one accuse he or she of being egotistical but quite the contrary; They will be bathed in the light of having committed the ultimate in selfless acts.

Then suddenly M was beside me holding up the unicorn and turning it in the candle-light. I was jolted out of my spiralling baby thoughts.

"Once around the room with the unicorn for good luck," she said smiling.

"You'll break her, I said (again), peering at closely at the glass unicorn.

Standing proudly, with one hoof raised provocatively, it was as if the unicorn was daring her to break it. She twirled it round her head making swishing noises.

"May we always have the luck of the Irish and the arrogance of the French," she chanted solemnly and we both burst out laughing.

"Now put her back up on the shelf, before you drop her… whisking the delicate little thing around like that," I said disapprovingly.

M tutted and placed it high up on a corner shelf above her bed next to a little green, carved, jade Buddha.

"She's tougher than she looks," she remarked under her breath.

Up on the shelf, the unicorn could barely be seen in the shadow. In the dark, her magic was gone.

The door buzzer went. I jumped, alarmed by the sudden intrusion. Other people. People I didn't know. What would they think of me? Would they all be like Kristiana?

M ran to the hallway, excited. Her first guest. Who would it be? Taru, one of M's students at the *Fac*? Etienne, an opinionated short guy from Paris? Kristiana, the self-obsessed photographer?

"Oh," called M from the doorway, reading my thoughts again. "Kristiana called, she can't make it after all, what a pity."

"*Quel dommage*!" I thought, suppressing a wide grin and secretly swelling with delight.

As it turned out, everyone turned up except Kristiana and that was a relief for me. Even M mumbled something under her breath about Kris being unreliable and this made me feel pleased. Perhaps M was getting the message after all. Perhaps she just needed some more time to make up her own mind about the Swiss Queen and her spider-eyes. Several of M's English students were there: Taru, a tall, thoughtful girl wearing too many beads, heavy turquoise earrings and a tie-dyed pink and flame-red sarong (she hadn't bothered to fancy dress according to her, but really no-one could tell). Angéline, a small, dark and very French-looking girl who spoke little English but with a smile that could melt the polar icecaps, so it hardly mattered. She kissed my hand on meeting then hugged me fiercely. She had decided to dress as a witch as well and wore a long, black, velveteen dress and white make-up. Angéline, however was, like myself, not convincing witch material. Rémy and Etienne were two short boys of about nineteen. Etienne was arrogant as hell, but this was obviously a thin veil intended to cover his insecurity and shortness. Still, knowing this didn't stop him being tiresome. Rémy was sweeter, quieter with big, solemn, brown eyes. Pools of eyes, I thought, in which you could happily lose yourself. There were a few others whose names I know but with whom I didn't really feel I got to know at all. Perhaps it was the language barrier or the general exuberance of the evening. There was one girl, Adèle, who looked like Cleopatra, or at least how Cleopatra is portrayed in the movies with rich, thick, dark hair, creamy skin and cat-like eyes. There was Jeanne, a black guy from Marseilles with bad skin, who was just visiting Angéline, and a spindly youth with ice-pale skin and long Jesus-like, curling brown locks. He was called Guy. And lastly a friend of Angéline, a shortish boy of about twenty called Marc who reminded me of Mr. Tumnus the faun from *The Lion the Witch and the Wardrobe*, due to the little tufts of goatee-type beard he proudly sported on the end of his chin and his delicately pointed shell-like pixie ears.

We started off, not in the Dark Café as arranged. In true M style there was an immediate and impulsive change of plan. Instead we headed, black dresses flapping in the wind and making us look like a troop of prehistoric birds, to L'Arabesque or, as it was more commonly referred to because there were internet computers there, the Cybercafé.

Once inside, the barmen were full of friendly banter.

"*Ah, M, encore bourrée!*" one of them called from behind the mirrored bar, giving us a toothy grin. M grinned widely. She was indeed getting a little bit drunk. The other brought pitchers of beer and chatted quickly and incomprehensively in French. I was sat beside Etienne, much to my annoyance. He kept on saying he did not understand my accent because it was so strong and harsh and horrible. I felt like smacking his smug effeminate little face but managed to be cool and ignore him.

M was thoroughly enjoying every moment. She was the centre of attention. The mentor of some of these kids, yet not much older than them. She was the older, wiser, cooler, living-away-from-home and confident grown-up. For an instant I saw her turn into Kristiana, then hastily dismissed that image.

After an hour or so in the Cybercafé listening to the French folk and rap fusion of Louise Attaque and getting extremely tipsy, if not a little, *bourrée*, Rémy quietly announced that we should move on to the Dark Café if we wanted seats. M tutted at his good sense but began immediately to gather everyone up and carry out his adult suggestion. I was already beginning to feel rather hazy, as if my brain cells were being replaced with cotton wool balls, and I made a mental note not to drink further alcohol that night. M grabbed my arm on the way out the door.

"Isn't it fun?" she said, grinning from ear to ear like the Cheshire cat, "Everyone is here and it's all going swimmingly."

"Swimmingly?" I asked, laughing, "where on earth did you get that word from? Not from Belfast," I said, jogging along beside her to catch up with her three league boots strides.

"*I* am no longer a Belfast-girl," she said, grinning more widely, "Belfast is like a dream, a childhood dream."

"Or a nightmare," I said knowing her thoughts.

Someone was running behind us. It was little Angéline, her velveteen flapping in the wind like a broken umbrella.

"Wait!" she cried, "*nous avons des vélos, c'est trop loin à pied.*"

"Nonsense!" answered M, sternly, "It's only a few kilometres," and she lengthened her stride as if to demonstrate the futility of the bicycle suggestion.

We sat at a long table in the Dark Café, having arrived, predictably, without the aid of bicycles. We ordered pitchers of strong Belgian beer and were all quite drunk by midnight. I had forgotten my mental note reminding me not to drink any more alcohol. I was in the middle of a long winded philosophical discussion with Rémy about life after death.

"I know that the answer is so obvious that we have all just overlooked it," he said earnestly, peering into his golden beer, his long curling sooty eyelashes sweeping downwards.

"It's like when you lose something and you look absolutely everywhere and still can't find it but you've missed it because it is right under your nose. You don't look in the most obvious place because in a way it's too obvious, in a way you are looking for something more complex, somewhere farther away, somewhere more hidden. Well, it's exactly the same when you are looking for an answer to life and death. Why are we here? What happens after we die? I bet it is right under our noses all the time and that is why nobody has discovered it. We are making it too complicated."

I nodded slowly, the beer slowing the rate at which my mind could absorb his words of wisdom but at the same time realizing that I had heard these words of wisdom somewhere before; they could be mine, actually.

"Like gravity," I said suddenly.

"Chapeau!" cheered Rémy and laughed. Then we both looked a bit puzzled because it wasn't really like gravity at all. But gravity was close to what we were trying to describe so it would have to suffice.

M was sitting next to Guy and running her fingers through his long, 'Jesus hair' and staring into his eyes. He was grinning like a loon. Depeche Mode was playing in the background. The French were up dancing jerkily and moodily. Suddenly a '*Jean-Jacques*' was standing in front of me. The *Jean-Jacques* is the French equivalent of the '*Knacker*' in Dublin or his Northern counterpart the '*Spiderman*' in Belfast. Uneducated and not too bright and badly dressed. The Jean-Jacques was sporting a mullet hairstyle, a military style moustache and was wearing a cut-off T-shirt and a pair of track suit bottoms with red and yellow flames running up the sides of them.

"*Est-ce que tu veux danser?*" The Jean-Jacques asked tentatively.

Dance? I wanted to dance right out the door when I saw you, I thought while busily preparing a civil reply in my head. There was the usual seconds of delay whilst I formed the sentence in French, checking for grammatical errors, correct locations of prepositions and general flaws and during which I probably looked as if I'd had a lobotomy. Speaking another language is no mean task. It reminded me a little of playing hockey. First of all you have all the rules which you must learn and follow at all times but in the meantime you must play the game, react spontaneously and be prepared to pass back as quickly as possible. If you don't, you lose your moment to act, as well as the ball to someone else and you are left standing there frustrated, knowing you could have done it but having worried so much about following the rules, standing in the correct position, not crossing the lines and so on, that you miss your golden opportunity to actually play.

Speaking another language is like this for me. Busy forming the sentence, checking for potential errors and recalling the correct vocabulary from the recesses of your mind takes time and then, just when it is ready to be spoken, the conversation matter changes. They have moved on to something else and your opportunity to voice your opinion has passed swiftly by. Then you have to start all over again with another sentence.

Once, at secondary school, our usual Physical Education teacher was off sick. We were all quite relieved for she was a notorious lesbian and all sorts of horror stories about her and certain first year gymnastics team members were rife in circulation. She was Miss Woods, bulging eyes like a frog and a large, nobly, red nose. Out she would stride in her warm fleecy track suit swinging her hockey stick, looking all warm and cosy and 'just-had-a-nice-hot-cup-of-coffee-thanks', whilst we stood in the biting January wind in above-the-knee navy wrap-over skirts and short sleeved white, airtex gym tops, knees knocking with cold and blue to match our skirts and fingers already numb from holding the sticks. Grumbling and shivering with nothing to look forward to except another hour of the hockey pitch, then a tepid communal shower in the scummy changing room which had a permanent odour of feta cheese and damp knickers.

But today was different. Instead of Miss Woods, we had Miss McGinnis. And at first we were suspicious. Could she be worse even? Would we be begging for the return of Miss Froggy Woods after half-an-hour's coaching by her replacement? We were to be pleasantly surprised.

As it turned out Miss McGinnis (call me Patty, girls), despite being full of the type of stoicism which is unpleasant in middle-aged women, with ruddy cheeks and a 'no nonsense' demeanour, she was a damn good teacher. "Ignore the rules for a moment girls," she sparkled, "play the damn game, get the damn ball and put it in the damn net." We were astounded and giggly. Miss Froggy Woods never said 'damn', only gosh and good lord and super. So for the first time in my life I actually played hockey. For the first time in my life I forgot about the rules, the lines, the off-side, who to pass to. I just ran like the wind and got that ball and ran like the wind again and put it in the net. The whistle blew, my team cheered. We had won. I had scored a goal. "A star," Patty sparkled and patted my back. Then she brought out trays of jaffa cakes on which we all munched feeling very pleased with ourselves and no-one more so than me.

Now, in the Dark Café, Reims, confronted with the Jean-Jacques and his flaming trousers, I wished I could forget the rules and run like the wind with my ball. I wished I could just speak it, spit out those words and if they were wrong, they were wrong. But whilst the sentence played on my lips and was tantalisingly close to being transformed from a thought to the actual spoken word Etienne butted in with his usual gracelessness.

"*Elle ne parle pas français,*" he said and rudely waved the Jean-Jacques away.

And with that he swung his short French arm around me and crossed his short French legs.

"*Elle est la mienne.*"

At this I almost choked on my beer which I had hastily lifted to aid the conduction of my prepared dialogue. I looked around for M or Rémy or someone to rescue me from these two horrors. M and Jesus were on the dance floor jerkily swaying to a Sergeant Garcia number.

"*En fait, cela n'est pas vrai, monsieur, je parle parfaitement le français mais je ne veux pas danser parce que je suis un peu fatiguée,*" I managed to blurt out quite nicely because I was so angry with Etienne. And it was partially true. I was a little bit tired.

I shoved him away.

The Jeans-Jacques shrugged.

"If you want to date French men then you have to learn to speak French," he said in staccato English, perhaps not comprehending my lovely and jubilantly delivered sentence or not having appreciated it fully. Then he sauntered off across the bar. We both laughed but I moved to Taru's table to evade the advances of Etienne's short, creeping limbs. I told her about my encounter and she smiled slowly and stretched luxuriously like a cat after a bowl of cream. She looked up at the ceiling dreamily.

"I love discoloured bulbs," Taru said thoughtfully and, as usual completely changing the subject to something more abstract.

I looked up thinking, why would you love discoloured bulbs? And besides they weren't discoloured at all. They were electric blue and shocking pink and Halloween orange. I looked at her questioningly, puzzled.

She pointed up again, "discoloured bulbs."

Then I got it. She meant 'these coloured bulbs'. We sat there staring at these coloured bulbs until they began to move and then the whole room began to spin and then I began to feel very nauseous. I found M and told her I was going back. She and Jesus just grinned at me from the dance floor. His head, silhouetted against a golden disco light behind him made him look like he had a halo. I swayed towards the door and went out, relieved into the luscious, wet, cool night air.

II

The damn phone was still ringing and ringing. In my dream I got up to answer it. In my dream I was an old, old lady who couldn't move very fast. My cat was asleep on my lap and I was annoyed at having to disturb her to answer the phone. I was irked. I tutted as I raised my creaky old bones off the couch and proceeded to the hallway with the aid of my stick. The ringing seemed more urgent now and I began to feel frightened. The hat stand made coat shadows on the wall, twisted scarecrows, hanging men, limbs dangling at unnatural angles. I looked to the door and through the rippled glass pane there. A small child was running away but, when he looked around, it was not a child but a dwarf, a child-sized body with the wizened head of an old man. He grinned at me in my dream. I clutched at the banister for support and my stomach lurched in fear. I reached out to lift the receiver to stop this invasion that is piercing my brains. To perhaps hear the voice of a friend, an ordinary kind voice would break this spell of fear. But I was very old in my dream. All my friends were dead. My heart was beating very fast now, each beat tumbling into the next. I finally touched the receiver but the ringing stopped. I heard a dull click as the caller hangs up. A bad omen, I think, in my dream.

But I could still hear the damn thing. I was awake now and in an unfamiliar place. But actually it wasn't the phone ringing. It sounded more like the door bell. I lifted my head and squinted to see if I could work out where I was and what was happening. I felt like I was underwater and slowly, painfully rising to the surface. My head hurt and was heavy. My eyes felt swollen and itchy and my mouth dry. Of course, now I start to remember. The party, the Dark Café, getting home in the early hours. Alone? Where were the rest, M and all her new friends? The ringing again, more like buzzing. 'Yes, yes,' I tried to say but the words didn't come out. I got up in slow motion and fumbled for the light switch but couldn't find it. I ran my hand along the wall, up and down, across. I still couldn't find it.

I tutted, impatient with myself. I trundled towards the hall on scissor legs with hands outstretched in anticipation of bumping into something. Finally, finally I found the intercom and after some further seconds wasted finding the right button I buzzed the door open. On retrospect this was a very stupid thing to do but I was too muddled for caution.

Kristiana was standing in the doorway her black spider eyes shining. M rushed in, her collar turned up against the wind and rain which was falling sideward and into the hall. Kristiana followed, a beatific smile on her face as the warmth and shelter reached her, eyes closed in relief.

"Hellish weather, Oh, I'm absolutely shattered," Kristiana said, sailing into the living room like a kite and shaking the cold raindrops from her coat. She and M smelled like the rain and the street and the wet grass outside. M flopped down on the sofa.

"Make coffee Charl, shweetie," she pleaded, waving a small pale mitt in the direction of the green kitchenette.

"I'm tired," I answered, feeling rather cross. "I've been asleep and you have woken me up at, how late is it?–Five-thirteen?" I glanced at the plastic travel alarm on the sideboard.

"Well you left early, we had a 'lock-in' at the Dark Café and drank on till about half an hour ago, you should have stayed, the amber nectar flowed all night, fantastic."

Suddenly I was too tired to be cross. I remembered leaving early and then crashing out in the flat and having that strange dream. I still had goose bumps.

"I'll make you coffee then I'm going back to bed and shall sleep the sleep of the unconscious and not wake up again till noon."

M smiled and snorted and closed her eyes, *"merci bien petite soeur."*

Kristiana got up and took off her coat which she slung carelessly over the back of the sofa. She began a slow waltz around the room, her spider eyes taking in all our things.

They slid over M's glass collection which was arranged above the sink on rickety green shelves. A precarious home for such a treasured collection, I thought. Small chunky shot glasses with 'Schulz' in gold lettering, smuggled furtively out of a café in Berlin. A 'White Guinness' pint glass from Temple bar in Dublin, a stemmed Belgian beer glass with a yellow 'Grimbergen' crest emblazoned on the side hastily tossed into an open bag on the floor of an Amsterdam coffee shop. M's leaky orange teapot sat on the drainer. There were plastic aubergine and paprika shaped pot hangers on the wall above the drainer from which scissors, a tea strainer and coloured plastic clothes pegs dangled. A novelty green violin bottle opener lay on the worktop. It was a cluttered normal rather lived-in kitchen and I felt sure that Kristiana would be disapproving of the musty yellow lino and the damp stains on the walls. It was all so working class to her. It smelled to her. I could almost see her trying not to wrinkle up her nose in disgust. I imagined her flat in Paris, all white and cream and minimalist. Emotionless, like her. A veneer of coldness and sterility. Ah, but what lies beneath Krissy? What lies beneath those high cheekbones and cold eyes? Just an insecure little girl trying to be somebody and impressing nobody. For a moment our eyes met and she looked quickly away as if reading my thoughts. For a moment she felt exposed and vulnerable. Then I looked away too, embarrassed by my own harsh judgment again.

"Oh," she said and laughed her Tinkerbell laugh, quickly and seamlessly wrapping herself up in the gloss again. "This flat is so sweet and....kitsch and...and intimate," she breathed. "I'll make the coffee." She glided into the kitsch kitchenette and noiselessly filled the tin kettle. Kristiana seemed incapable of walking anywhere. She glided, sailed and floated. Head high, moving gracefully. No sudden jerking movements broke her harmonious gait. She never stumbled or tripped or suddenly lost the power of one knee finding herself thrown unceremoniously off balance. Nothing broke the symphonic flow of Kristiana in motion.

I sat down beside M, her eyes were still closed and her lilac eyelids quivered slightly, like butterfly wings. The Halloween make-up was long worn off. They looked so soft and delicate. I had the feeling that if I touched one with my fingertip that the lilac colour would come off and smudge like a palette of expensive creamy eye shadow.

Kristiana came out with two mugs of Nescafé. She sat down opposite us.

"I know this is hard for you," she said suddenly and maternally, losing her superior air.

I looked into her dark eyes. Hard for me? What did she mean? Leaving my home? Being here in France? Why the sudden concern? The simple statement confused and upset me and I couldn't ask her what she meant and I couldn't reply. It all seemed complicated and besides I didn't wish to discuss my innermost feelings and fears with her no matter how caring she was trying to be. I looked at my wee sister lying asleep on the sofa, thumbs tucked into palms just as they are in the womb.

"I understand," she said nodding wisely, "it's difficult."

"Maybe I *could* talk to this girl", I thought. This spider-eyed, chestnut-haired, sailing girl. Maybe together we could crack her sparkling pristine shell and get to the underside, the raw belly, where her fears scuttled around in dark corners. Maybe we could get to my depths as well and break down that barrier of bravado that M and I both carried around so well, covering the sensitivity and the hurt with a shining banner of self-assurance. Except my banner was not as high nor shining as hers. Mine flapped and waned in a wind of uncertainty and self-doubt. Maybe she needed me to see her real self or maybe I needed to show her mine. But I was not ready. We were too different.

I come from a place Krissy where every street corner sports a group of youths wearing baseball caps and carrying knives. They hang out outside the local off-license or video library. People who live their whole lives in a narrow corridor of half light. Seventeen-year-old mothers shuffle to the takeaway in bedroom slippers, smoking cigarettes, never aspiring to anything more than a new couch or the latest colour TV model or a holiday in Costa Brava where the bars all serve English Breakfasts all day and the waiters spit in the milky tea.

I come from a place where people are blissfully unaware of the outside world. They live and die in stream of shabby consumerism and ingrained tribalism, experiencing nothing, learning nothing, knowing nothing. Uneducated, uncultured and unseeing. I come from a place where paramilitary thugs act like a police force. They have shaven heads and cock them sideways at things they don't understand, the way a dog would, curious but without the capacity to understand something different, another viewpoint or another way of life. I come from a place, Krissy, where everyone eats strawberry-flavoured jam but no-one has ever tasted a real strawberry. I tasted the strawberry when I left Belfast and there is no going back to the fake chemical stuff. It is addictive and exhilarating and you can't switch it off. But somehow it is also sad because once you've tasted the real fruit you can never again be easily contented with another version of it. Once the light has been switched on you can never be contented with the half-light. Without the light there is no dark. Without the dark there is no light. Yin and Yang.

You see Krissy, you and I are very different and I can't be your friend. You grew up having ballet lessons and listening to Bach and Mozart and Puccini. You grew up on an oak polished floor with a grand piano in the drawing room. You spent Sundays after church trotting around a paddock on a pony. Your parents bought coffee beans and knew which red wines to serve with beef and which whites to serve with lemon sole. You were learning three languages by the time you were able to talk and practising *pliers* at the bar in a polished wooden hall on Saturday mornings. At the same time, me and M were poking dead wasps around a jam jar full of sticky water.

I smiled politely at her but said nothing. We drank our coffee in exhausted silence. Kristiana left at six to catch the early Paris train and I went back to my mattress on the floor. M slept on the sofa. I dreamed no more of being old and afraid but wondered about my future. As always there was the uneasiness and uncertainty.

The days rolled into each other. M went to the *Fac* every morning. I slept late and got up when the autumn sun was high in the sky. I thought, I should be working, but then thought no more of it. I opened the little wooden hatch above where I slept and let in a cold draft of air. It was bright and bitter cold. Maybe it would snow soon and I could wake up to muffled street sounds and black trees dusted with icing sugar frost.

Chapter 4 – By the canal

Although I wasn't working, I was filling my days with ease and getting into a slower more relaxed pace of life. I was enjoying doing little things. Even cleaning the flat gave me little pleasures. I'd put on loud music and shout tunelessly along to Sinead O' Connor, Bjork or PJ Harvey. Then I'd assemble all the cleaning products on the worktop and begin to dust, polish, scrub and vacuum. I even took great pains to make an air-freshener using a plastic plant spray bottle filled with water and adding lavender oil.

Washing was a pain because it had to be done in the bath, then wrung out by hand and dried either out the window on the ledge on a collapsing plastic clothes drier or on the living room radiator which made the rooms steamy and damp. But hard work or not I was infused with energy. And I was by myself doing my own thing. I felt free and thought I could go on like this indefinitely, but of course I couldn't. My savings, I had calculated over and over again and still they would only stretch to five or six months at most and that was without paying rent. So whilst I soaked tired patterned yellow cushion covers in the bath or dusted M's glass collection I fantasised about getting a well paid-job which paid the rent of a parquet-floored apartment with French doors that opened onto a walled, sunny courtyard and still having enough money left over for restaurant dinners and nights out in Paris.

After the cleaning I would go shopping. I have never particularly enjoyed shopping but shopping in France when you have all day to do it, was quite a luxury. The range of fruits and flowers, fresh fish, coffees, teas and cakes in little quaint individual shops were delightful. The fact that you could go to a different shop for each item on your list would be a pain for most working people but for me it was a feast for the senses. First the greengrocer's for an aubergine, a courgette, some fresh red tomatoes for tonight's ratatouille and I couldn't resist the bunch of lavender to hang by the window. Then, the Boulangerie for oven fresh, still warm, bread and a little chat in my tentative French with the red-cheeked lady at the counter. It didn't seem to bother her that I didn't understand her life story after the first "*Alors..c'est formidable...mon mari..pah....*blah blah blah," she just wanted to tell it, so I stood nodding at appropriate intervals and smiling sweetly, reddening slightly as I felt such a fraud, while she wrapped my baguette and hot pain au chocolats. I dawdled after that to window-shop. All the Halloween paraphernalia was gone and I enjoyed the neutral interlude before the Christmas decorations would go up. Soon every shop would be twinkling soft lights out into the wet, dark streets and windows would be stuffed with Santas, reindeers and elves. I popped in to a little shop named Rêves du Jours and came out with three strawberry and cinnamon candles and some 'energy' incense sticks. I really wanted to try their little bags of mixed dried herbs entitled 'Sleep Easy' as I'd been having such troubled dreams but I thought I was spending too much already and I still had to buy some rum, honey and limes for some of M's students who might have popped round later for English conversation classes, or more realistically, sitting around on cushions mumbling a few sentences in English then getting drunk and speaking French all evening.

Then I spied some gorgeous sunflowers with their huge heads nodding in the breeze. How lovely I thought, sunflowers and bunches of lavender and strawberry candles whilst sipping rum and honey and maybe the cushion covers and rugs would be dry and sweet-smelling by tonight. The flat would be lit up by candlelight and if it rained we would hear the urgent drumming on the roof reminding us that we were all cosy and dry. I looked at my watch. It was half past four. If I dashed to the supermarket and got the honey and limes, I could dash back and get the sunflowers and the rum on the way home, then catch an hour's reading before starting to cook and still have time to decorate with the lavender and candles and things.

But, as luck would have it, I had a long queue in the supermarket and by the time I got back to the flower kiosk it was shut and the sunflowers were looking at me accusingly from behind the glass. They looked sad that no-one had bought them. It reminded me of the time in my childhood when I had persuaded my mummy to buy me a watch because it had a sad face and was staring out of the shop window somehow willing me to take it home. We did. But then I had cried with relief and when I explained to my mummy why, she got cross and was going to make me take it back. I got to keep the watch with the sad face in the end but there ensued a lengthy lecture on the difference between animate objects and inanimate objects. A watch had no feelings because it did not actually exist. It was there but not actually existing like a person or an animal. It was not alive. So it was dead then? I had asked, even more troubled by the sad face but beginning to see why it had looked so sad. It hadn't wanted to die at all. But it had gradually dawned on me that things like dolls and watches and pictures could not feel and, therefore, I shouldn't extend my empathy to them as I did to dogs and cats and rabbits in hutches and monkeys in cages in the zoo.

I was taken to the zoo only once as a child because I had cried myself to sleep every night for months afterwards. In the 1970s, when I was growing up, zoos were not open, spacious and as natural as possible, as they are today. There were tigers and bears walking up and down in small cages, swinging their huge proud heads and pressing their noses against the bars in misery. I could hear them inside my head. They said, "let me out, I can't get out," and how I wanted to but I was a powerless little girl in a dress made from an old curtain with pink and navy-blue swirls and I was crying and my tears and snotters mixed were running into my ice cream making it warm and salty; the whole world was a blur and I wished it could be me in that cage instead of the bear or the tiger or the wretched little spider monkey who was hugging and rocking himself in the corner of his smelly cage amongst rotten bits of banana and droppings. M watched me curiously from her pram, luckily still oblivious to the suffering of animals. Raspberry sauce from her ice cream had made two lines of red run down from the corners of her mouth making her look like a little vampire.

I realised I had been day dreaming again and turned from the flower shop window towards Rue des Epinards which branched onto Rue du MC Fouriérès where we lived. Then I suddenly had a brain wave. Of course! Down by the canal were these tall yellow flowers that looked a bit like the flowers on a gorse bush and were complete weeds but I could pick a bunch and have lovely bright yellow after all and forget my sad sunflowers trapped in their vase behind glass. I hitched up my shopping bags and headed the opposite direction. It was getting dark but it wouldn't take me long if I could remember exactly where they were.

It was darker by the canal than on the street and the water looked black and foreboding. I felt the first twinge of regret. This was a stupid idea. Who needed yellow flowers anyway? But here I was and in a few minutes I could cross the bridge, gather an armful of the tall bright weeds and be back on the street in five minutes. I glanced behind me as I always did in the dark. I could see the lights of the shop windows and hear cars rattle past. I felt a cold wet drop on my nose. It was starting to rain. I took a deep breath and walked briskly across the bridge.

In the distance I could just about make out where the yellow flowers should be. They were about twenty meters away, by a crumbling wall which surrounded a derelict cottage. The flowers I wanted were an extension of that garden, spilling out onto the canal path. The garden itself harboured a whole tangle of sweet smelling delights like raspberry and blackberry bushes and the end of the summer roses in their faded glory. Gorgeous, pallid, blue hydrangea poked out from a rabble of stinging nettles. Ivy, tall grasses and privet hedge stirred in the breeze. I turned left towards the cottage. The wind began to blow harder. Cold, cruel gusts that drove the rain into my face. My hands, gloveless, were freezing carrying these plastic bags of shopping and it was almost night now. I could only make out shapes and shadows. No moonlight tonight. The heavy Northern French cloud had put paid to that.

But suddenly there they were. The tall yellow weeds which looked a bit like foxgloves but with less delicate bell-like petals, smaller and more closely strewn together up and down the stem. Are they called golden rain? I couldn't remember. The stem itself was more fibrous, woody. I set my bags down gladly and rubbed my sore hands together to bring back the circulation. I knelt down meaning to pick four or five of the long stems and dash back to the light and safety of the street. I wanted to get away quickly from this twilight canal side. I felt frightened now as I bent down. As if I was being watched. My heart beat like a scared rabbit cornered by an enthused hunting dog. I wanted to move quickly, get the damn flowers and go but I felt sure that, by moving, I would draw attention to myself and that whoever was watching, would see me.

"Get a grip girl," I commanded myself sternly, "There is no-one here but you, no-one in their right mind would be by the canal in the dark in a pending storm. It's just your overactive imagination kicking in like it always does."

I heard a noise in the bushes in front of me and jerked my head up but it was just the wind. My hands were trembling now as I tugged and twisted at the fibrous stems but they would not break. As well as their toughness they were covered in tiny thorns so my hands were cut to pieces and stinging as well as cold and wet.

Again there came a rustle in the bush just ahead of me behind the stone wall. Maybe it was a stray dog or cat. Or maybe the wicked witch who lives in the cottage, Charlotte, you mad thing. I asked myself. Or maybe the 'no-one in their right mind' whose image I'd summoned up earlier during my courage-fortifying self lecture. This phrase was one I wished I had not used.

Later on, when I was safely installed at home sipping rum and honey and listening to the fluffy French pop tunes of Air and Stereolab, this would all seem funny or like some strange dream. Oh how I wished I was there already. Damn! The rustle again, louder now. This time I stood up and turned around.

"*Il y a quelqu'un?*" I called weakly. *Was* there anybody there? My voice was hardly audible above the wind and the rain, falling faster now, wetter, huge fat drops, more urgent. I looked beyond the bush to the deserted cottage and my heart flipped over in my chest.

There was a light at the window. And someone moved in there.

But this was the derelict cottage. Who would be there at night? The roof was missing as were half the walls. The whole place was crumbling and decaying. The garden had invaded the house through the cracked door and window frames and was taking over. Ivy crept silently up the walls, winding itself around the brickwork in intricate patterns. There was no protection from the elements in there. Rain, hail and snow fell in through the roof. But maybe a tramp or homeless person seeking some form of shelter from the sudden storm. Yes that was it, I convinced myself. Some wino who was drunk by the canal at dusk was caught suddenly out in the open by the storm and seeking at least shelter from the wind had gone into the old ruined house.

I strained to see further, some evidence of my self-sedating little fairy tale. Suddenly I wasn't sure if I'd seen a light at the window or not. Maybe it had been a trick of the eyes. After grovelling about in a bush for a few minutes, maybe when I looked up it had looked light because of course it was lighter and higher up at the window than down in the undergrowth. Yes, a trick of the light or what little there was, multiplied by my imagination. Suddenly I didn't care anymore, about the tramp or the light or the damn yellow flowers which refused to be uprooted. I was leaving.

I gathered up my two plastic carrier bags and cursed the flowers. They nodded their heavy yellow heads at me, shaking their heavy yellow bells in the wind. They were sending me away. Reprimanding me for trying to take them away from their home and imprison them in a glass tower in a stuffy room full of cigarette smoke and the burnt toffee smell of decade-old, oven grease which infused the atmosphere of M's place. They hated me for trying to steal them away from their canal side, away from the flat, sleeping barges and the sweet, luscious rain. I was guilty. I was just as guilty as those men who capture monkeys, gibbons and chimpanzees from their tropical bedrooms in the trees and take them to Europe to live out the rest of their days in a metal box with, perhaps, a bolt through their head. A laboratory specimen. No more life. Just alive. A thing of suffering and misery. But surely flowers are different? They are not sentient? Surely it isn't cruel to pick them and put them in a vase for your own whimsical pleasure? I didn't know. How could I know if they could feel my fingernails digging into the tough flesh of their stems? Their veins, bleeding green sap on to my frozen hands. How could I know if they were screaming in agony in a language I didn't understand or care to? Animate, inanimate? Where does a flower fit in? I didn't even want them anymore and for sure I had destroyed them by twisting and torturing their stems. But they nodded to me as if they had won this time.

I turned away and breathed deeply the wetness and sweetness of the heavy rain. It was actually beautiful here by the canal, in the storm. But also frightening. I glanced back to the cottage. Definitely no light now. No-one. Just blackness. I started towards the bridge, my heartbeat pounding in my temples. I tried to cheer myself with images of the prospective evening. M running round in the green kitchen, lighting candles, mixing the ratatouille, adding the sour cream, chopping the garlic and pouring the wine. I could almost smell the basil, thyme and oregano mingled with the many ancient burnt-in smells from the old oven. I was hungry as well as tired, drenched and scared. I quickened my pace, head down against the wind. I looked up briefly as I neared the place where I was to cross the bridge. From nightmare land to reality, light, warmth and security. But then my stomach turned to ice.

There was a hooded figure on the bridge.

When I told M about this later, she looked at me thoughtfully and then said it must have been a premonition, some kind of omen. She didn't think I was crazy or having hallucinations or just making something up to make my day seem more exciting. When we were all sat around the floor on cushions drinking wine and rum and nibbling Reims special champagne biscuits (on which you could easily break a tooth), it did, as I had earlier suspected all seem like a queer dream or something I had read about, happening to someone else.

Taru was sympathetic and philosophical. Rémy fixed his large dark eyes on me and gulped down his rum. M looked paler than usual. Etienne laughed and made ghost noises whilst catching appreciative glimpses of himself in a small television screen which was always switched off because it didn't work.

"I'm not trying to scare you," I said.

"I know," she answered, then paused.

"And actually, it's pretty cool," she smiled and brushed imaginary crumbs from her jeans.

"Or maybe I have a doppelganger here in Reims."

"But I did think it was you on that bridge," I said peering into the bottom of my glass of rum feeling suddenly hot and embarrassed. M was rearranging her cigarettes and lighter on the floor in front of her. The heavy rain beat down on the roof. The little window overlooking a crumbling courtyard was open slightly to let out the smoke and two weary cacti leaned against it as if gasping for air or freedom. A dog barked down below. I was beginning to feel normal again. The way you do after waking up from a frighteningly realistic dream. The first few moments that you are still in the dream, awake but believing it, heart pounding, in limbo between the world of the mind and the world of the body. Then gradually the dream lifts and floats off leaving only intangible fragments. The ability to recall the intensity of those moments dissipating as the day wears on and as the daily activities take over. I felt silly now recalling the twilight canal side, my struggle to get the yellow flowers, my imagining the light and movement at the window of the old cottage and my panic and taking flight across the bridge. It was beginning to seem grainy. It had taken on a surreal quality.

Taru poured herself another rum and crept over beside me. Her large grey eyes were intently curious. She arranged her tall frame cross-legged on a yellow cushion, her broad back against the wall. She pulled up the sleeves of her Icelandic-patterned jade and turquoise jumper revealing slim brown wrists and a thin sinew of dark leather which was wrapped around one. French wrists, I thought. Irish wrists would be slightly chunky, pale and mottled with freckles, Celtic skin. Papery skin. Warrior skin. Taru began to roll a cigarette from the pack of Drum in the centre of the floor. A calmness fell upon the room. The loud, inaccurate plastic clock ticked on regardless. Etienne ceased his bleating laughter and rolled on to his back with his short French legs crossed and his head on Rémy's lap.

"Tell us what you saw," Taru said.

So I began. I told all the details from the shopping expedition to the sunflowers I couldn't buy then about my mad idea to pick some by the canal. About the feeling I had that someone was watching me. The light at the window, everything.

Then I told them that I had seen a figure on the bridge. And why had that scared me so much? It could have been someone out walking a dog, or a boy waiting for his lover to show up. There were any number of ordinary explanations. But I had been scared and I had wanted to run. The figure was neither male nor female. It had a hood up over its head.

It was looking into the water. It was slightly leant over. Its belly was pressed against the iron railings. It looked as if it had lost something in there or was calling to someone in there. And as I approached it, heartbeats now tumbling into one another in an irregular rhythm, it turned its head slowly and looked at me.

And it was my sister.

Her luminous white face shining in the grainy darkness. Her button nose and the shape of her round jaw I could make out though her eyes were just pools of shadow. But it was her. I smiled, relieved, then confused. What was she doing here? Looking for something, looking for me? She didn't know I was down here. Why should I be down here?

"M," I said, my voice piping and wavering,"What the hell are you doing here?"

I stepped closer and then, suddenly, gasped because it wasn't her at all. The jaw line was squarer, the nose was longer, the hair was dark. The figure looked at me briefly, then turned back to the water and continued to peer in.

I marched past, mumbled a sorry and then began to run across the bridge. I didn't look back. I dared not look back. That person , whoever it was, was giving me the creeps. Standing on a canal bridge in a storm freaking me out. I couldn't even tell if it was male or female. Why had it looked like my sister? I must be going crazy.

That was it. I stopped and everyone was looking at me.

The small group stared at me for a while then a low murmur trickled into the silent and hushed concentration. Etienne broke the spell by getting up to use the toilet and flushing it noisily with the door open thus bringing us all immediately back to earth. Taru was nodding slowly.

"You had a premonition," she said.

"There is a message there from the other side, maybe a warning, I don't know."

"It's nonsense," M said, pulling a leg up under her and grinning wickedly. "You just smoked too much hash last night and imagined it all."

"No," Taru said, "My grandmother knows of these things, she has seen the other side too, in coffee grounds and in visions".

"Your grandmother hasn't even seen the other side of Reims," Etienne chimed in, settling down again and reaching for the now almost empty rum bottle.

Taru flashed him a severe look.

"Once, when we were mushroom picking, my grandmother and I, she told me a very strange story."

"Your granny and you went mushroom picking in the woods and started tasting the magic ones," M said, joining in the banter.

Taru smiled slowly and warmly. Taru was also affectionately known as 'mushroom woman'. She was always wandering around the woods, collecting different fungi, drying them, drawing them, recording them. She had a little book with records of the different types she had found and was also known to have sampled a few of them of them, noting the physical and psychological results. But Taru claimed to know the really dangerous ones. Knowledge which was passed on from her granny. She also knew the most powerfully hallucinogenic ones.

"Your granny is a witch and so are you," Etienne piped up.

Taru smiled, quite enjoying playing her mysterious self. A part she played so well because it wasn't acting at all; it was really her. Taru was too tall to be French and too blond. She was from German descent. She should have been awkward and clumsy and wishing she was like those small, dainty, dark-haired French women who enjoyed shopping so much and giggling as they clicked along shiny cobbled streets. Growing up to marry small dark French boys with slightly bandy legs who they had gone to school with and who had slightly too-long noses and would drive to work in 'companies' in red Fiats wearing collars and ties and smoking bitter-sweet smelling Gauloise cigarettes. Taru should have wanted these things, wanted to fit in. To marry and breed and fulfil all the rolls society demanded from a girl. But she didn't. She carried her tall frame and her differences proudly and seemed to glow with an inner light of calmness, tranquillity and peace, bathing luxuriously in her eccentricity. Taru could spend hours translating French poetry into English or German with an infinite patience and stern concentration, not giving up until it was perfect, even if it meant sitting up all night. She could spend days, meticulously threading little beads onto a thin string to make a necklace or a bracelet. She delighted in tiny, intricate things that other people often miss out on in their everlasting rush to fulfil some meaningless duties. She could stare at into the face of a dead fly or wasp, wondering how it sees, hears, how it feels, imagining what it is like to ride inside that fragile, wafer-like body, floating on the breeze. She could examine flower petals, endlessly stroking the velvet, marvelling at the patterns underneath, inhaling the rich sweet scents. Now she was standing up and stretching her long golden limbs.

"I must go," she said, bending over to collect her paraphernalia, "that story is for another day."

Etienne rolled his eyes. "We probably already heard it anyway".

Taru smiled enigmatically. "You cover your heart with a cobweb."

He looked puzzled but said nothing then farted loudly.

M and I tidied up when everyone left. It was around half past one in the morning and I was yawning like crazy. The whole canal drama seemed far away now and somehow silly. I wished I hadn't told it to anyone now. M got up to lock the door and turned to me flashing a big malicious grin.

"We'd better lock the door tonight in case your doppelganger tries to get in," she teased.

I laughed because I was more relaxed now and it didn't seem important any more.

M had always been braver than me. I was still scared of the dark. She revelled in it. I couldn't watch a horror movie on TV by myself, even a cheesy American one, without turning all the lights in the house on and creeping like a thief upstairs, heart pounding, starting at every noise, real or imagined, looking behind me, expecting to see the shadow of the axe murderer stalking me or meeting the mad eyes of an escaped lunatic. M was not that easily frightened.

I began to think about one of our camping trips and how I'd been terrified, lying in my thin sleeping bag shivering and listening to the noises of the woods one night and how my imagination had paralyzed me with fear while M slept on like an innocent babe in the woods.

We had camped in the woods whilst on holiday in Donegal one year, on a whim after stopping there accidentally and finding a magnificent lake surrounded by dark, tall evergreens. There were three of us, M, me and our friend, Michael, who was a tall, gaunt and rather effeminate guy who was fancied himself as a bit of a poet. The water itself was black and murky and ice cold. The wind was whispering through the trees, hushing us. It had reminded me of a childhood story called *The Enchanted Wood* by Enid Blyton, wherein three children had discovered a magical forest full of whispering trees and impossibilities. It was cool and dark in the wood and silent. So silent that our voices seemed to travel for miles when we spoke, then come back at us sounding strange and alien, frightening us a little. The forest floor was thick and soft as a feather duvet from layers of shed pine needles and it muffled all the sounds around us the way snow does.

It was fabulous running around, gathering wood for a fire, as even summer evenings in Ireland are chilly. We cooked beans in the scummy camping pot and teased each other whilst the low sun dappled our faces through the heavy canopy of branches. Then the sun had gone down.

We had the usual cool but not cold beers. Michael was talking but no-one was listening to his insecure prattle and artistic propelled angst. He was, according to himself, standing at a cross roads in his life and couldn't decide which road to take, terrified of making the wrong decision, peering ahead first down one path then the other. On the one hand he wanted to create art; write poetry or paint or compose a beautiful piece of music, all three things which he, by the way and in my opinion, was perfectly capable of. But on the other hand he wanted to contribute to the easing of the suffering of others and saw himself as some sort of Mother Theresa figure, unselfish, giving and completely altruistic. Bathed in a holy light. I could only ever imagine him poised at a desk in a chilly attic in the 19th century, quill in hand, anguishing over some unfinished ode or sonnet.

The fire was crackling away nicely and actually giving off some heat. M was busy sawing a rather sturdy branch which was too large for the fire with the mini-saw on her Swiss army knife, giving herself blisters, sweat beads popping out on her milk-white, dirt-smudged forehead. Her thin mouth was pursed into a straight line of effort and concentration. I was just content to absorb the night air and the satisfaction that we were far away from other people. The nearest village, (if you could call two bars and a post office a village), was forty-five minutes walk away on narrow country roads without lights. The damp firewood made popping and snapping noises like giant Rice Krispies, before succumbing to the flame.

Around midnight, or maybe later, we decided to go to sleep. Michael put out the fire rather unceremoniously by urinating on it and we clambered into the tent. There were a few minutes of blindness and confusion as we fumbled around for sleeping bags, falling on top of rucksacks, plastic bottles and other camping paraphernalia before we eventually found them and slid deliciously in, giggling and shivering with cold. Drifting off to sleep finally, I thought I heard voices but dismissed them as the tricks your mind plays on you in the limbo between being awake and being asleep.

Then I heard a scream.

It pierced the silence as if it had entered from a portal to another world. An unholy shriek. I was suddenly so shocked and so terrified that I could only lie there in the dark. My thoughts jumbling around in my head. I had insufficient organisation and co-odination to get them into a coherent pattern. What seemed like whole minutes passed, then Michael, in a weak, wavering and barely audible voice piped.

"Did you just hear someone scream?"

I answered in a whispery croak. We lay there for an immeasurable amount of time in a vacuum of fear, trapped in our own terrified bodies. I could hear Michael's irregular breathing. I didn't know what to do or even if I could move to do anything. No plans had been discussed in the event of such an emergency. Only the scissors which lay under my improvised pillow had been purposefully put there in case a fire made it necessary for us to cut our way out. Maybe they could be used as a weapon. Against whom? Or what? I could only think that I had no idea where my boots were and that the car keys were in my coat which was also lost in the black jumble of tent contents. Should we switch on the torch? Then we would draw attention to ourselves. Then the 'who' or the 'what' would see us and come for us too. The dark was our friend, our cloak of invisibility. The car was at least ten minutes walk from where we were camped. Ten minutes walk in the dark woods, the low branches scratching our faces, stumbling over fallen wood, orientation distorted by panic. Someone or something seeking us out. Something that could see in the dark.

Then we heard nearby footfalls. Michael told me later that, at that point he had nearly lost control of his bowels. Mine lurched and rolled. I sat up and scrambled for the tent flap. That was it, I was going. Maybe I stood a chance if I ran to the car (minus keys?) and without boots but I for sure wasn't sitting in that tent for one more second.

More footfalls, faster, then another scream. I yelped. Michael sat up too and we bumped heads in the darkness, in our panic. Then I felt his hand on my back.

"Shhh!" he said, "wait, listen."

I did, another scream, but...then laughter close by and more shouts and shrieks from farther away, then the splash of water in the distance. Suddenly it dawned on us. Michael was now giggling uncontrollably like a teenage girl. I knew he had his hand over his mouth because it was muffled.

"It's some kids mucking about in the lake after the pub," he gulped, lying back down in his sleeping bag and rolling with laughter. Adrenalin-induced hysterical laughter.

"It's OK kid, we are saved."

I lay down again and felt all the tension and fear drain out of me like water rushing downhill. I started to giggle.

I had what M called the *Slapen lachen* in German, or the 'sleeping laughter' as it is literally translated but it just means the nervous giggles.

"Shh!" Michael said again, "we'll waken the wee one."

I looked at the lumpy shape cocooned in the sleeping bag that was my sister. She was sound asleep and snoring softly. She hadn't heard a thing!

We giggled about this story as we had many times before. M said she wished she had my imagination and hyper-sensitivity. I cursed it and wished I had her confidence and fearlessness.

"I wouldn't have gone back into that wood that night for anything on earth once I'd gotten out of it," I said snuggling down under the quilt.

"What about me?" M asked in a faked quivery voice.

I lay there in the silence, deliberately not answering for a protracted moment to make it seem like I had to really think this one over. Of course I knew the answer. My sister was probably the only person on earth who could have gotten me deeper into the wood that night. If she'd been in any danger I wouldn't have hesitated. I would have gone out there and faced whatever demons roam the woods of Western Ireland. Silky haired banshees, wicked faeries, mad axe murderers, leering psychopaths. I would have faced them all for M. And she knew it.

"Oh, I would have gone back into the woods for you *shweetie*," I said.

M sighed and turned over.

"That's OK then, just checking," she said, yawning.

I closed my eyes again and for some reason they were full of tears.

Chapter 5 – By the pond

I

The next day I woke at eight o'clock. M was already up and on her *portable.* I could tell by her tone that she was excited.

"Yes, yes, I'd love to, that sounds too good to be true," she was saying whilst rushing around the kitchen, opening and closing the fridge and smoking a cigarette the way people smoke when they are on a mobile telephone, drawing and exhaling exaggeratedly.

I looked out the window. It was very windy. Blustery. Loose autumn leaves were blowing frantically up against the window then falling helplessly to the garden below, only managing to tap the window weakly before tumbling exhausted onto the ground.

I thought about going to look for a job at the *Fac* today. It was really time I was doing something. The vacation was losing its novelty. In fact, it was becoming tedious having no structure to my days. What had started out initially to be a long, golden stretch of free time and self discovery was turning into a gloomy, jobless and penniless landscape. I saw myself melodramatically in a Dali painting surrounded by desert and melting, weeping clocks. Time melting away.

M hung up. She was flushed and beaming from ear to ear.

"I have to go," she said grabbing her coat. "I'll tell you about it later. I tell you what, I'll see you in The Cybercafé at two for a coffee, then, I'll tell you the *bizz*."

And off she went into the wind. I glanced around the little flat. It looked dusty. Suddenly something caught my eye. But actually something caught my eye which was more noticeable by its absence than its presence. High up on the glass shelf, above M's bed, there was a space beside the jade, carved Buddha incense holder.

The unicorn was missing.

I began to look for it. It may have fallen onto the floor. I crawled on all fours to see under the bed. I found only crumpled up, fragrant socks and enormous, mutant dust bunnies. I checked under the small coffee table, lifted up the cushions, even my mattress but I could not find it anywhere. I felt a little bit sad. It was a beautiful thing and it conjured up an image of me and M on the train heading towards new adventures together. For me, the little glass unicorn represented our kinship and friendship and the beauty and fragility of life. It was our talisman. Maybe she had moved it somewhere safer, I thought. It certainly wasn't here. I made a mental note to ask her about it over coffee later.

I decided to run myself a bath and finish my book then maybe go out and have a look around Fnac or Galeries Lafayette, do some mindless shopping. Maybe I could procrastinate about the job hunting until tomorrow. Then the phone was ringing. I picked up M's portable. It smelled like banana and coconut, like Taru and summer. There was an audible click as the person on the other end hung up.

Later in the afternoon I was sitting in the Cybercafé nursing a Leffe beer and gazing out of the window. The soft, rhythmic melodies of Louise Attaque were playing in the background, a sort of mellow Brittany, folk mix with some French lyrics rapped out rather than sung. They had been playing it also on Halloween night. I liked it. It sounded like France. I felt rested and wistful and dreamy like the way you feel after long periods of sleep deprivation before you finally drift off into oblivion, powerless to stop it. I felt blissful and somehow windblown.

It was half past two and there was no sign of M. I wasn't bothered as she was often late. It was quiet and empty in the Cybercafé and no-one was bothering me, nor talking to me or even looking at me in the way that the French do, unabashed, staring and direct eye contact which always made me feel uncomfortable. I debated ordering another beer and reneged for lack of the motivation to move to the bar or summon Lucien who was busy polishing his glasses. M told me he was married with two children and lived in Troyes but had a mistress in Reims who he unashamedly paraded around on his arm. A tall gawky red-headed creature with stick limbs, a pot belly and round shoulders. And apparently, though I was never unfortunate enough to hear it, a laugh that could guide in ships on a stormy night such was its volume. I could only imagine how the wife looked if he found this individual appealing. Lost in my thoughts, I daydreamed on. Such was the privilege of the unemployed.

Suddenly M and Kristiana glided past the window. M taking long purposeful strides, head bent against the relentless autumn wind. Kristiana was talking and laughing. Her glorious chestnut hair whirling around her head in a halo of self-satisfaction. She was wearing a cream-coloured pashmina which she had wrapped tightly around her shoulders against the cold. She sailed past the window like a cream kite. M marched bravely beside her, eyes screwed up and a concentrated smile on her face. Hair flying around head, slightly dirty and dark blond.

I jumped up to leave and then sat down again. Hang on, I thought. It was already a quarter-to-three. M was supposed to meet me there at two. Why had she marched past?

She had obviously forgotten. She had obviously met Kristiana and found something much more interesting to do than to spend the afternoon with her dull sister. I suddenly felt very hurt. My stomach sank. I felt small, like the little sister following the big one and her big friends but unwanted and bothersome like a hanger-on. Just an uninteresting shape in the background, almost invisible, but there to be put up with and tolerated yet ignored. Part of me wanted to run after them but my pride wouldn't let me. Part of me wanted to forgive her for forgetting me, run after them and say, 'Hey, you're late, come into the café and have a drink, the two of you.' But I couldn't. It would be a poor show. A thin veneer. My voice would crack and waver, my lack of confidence would outshine my bravado and Kristiana would know how little I was feeling. She would smirk and say. 'Oh you poor thing, we completely forgot about you, M was so full of her *exposés* to mark. We were so busy this morning, what a day we've had.'

And M would smile and look at her watch and apologise and they would sail on in the wind like a brave ship with me trailing behind.

Lucien was talking to me from the bar, "*C'est ta soeur, non?*"

I smiled weakly and got up to leave, "*Oui c'est vrai,*" I answered and went outside into the late afternoon.

Easy tears stung my eyes and I wandered around the park. I found a bench by the town duck pond and watched the ducks bobbing and preening and diving for algae. I felt flat and wounded. I was too sensitive, too easily hurt, too ready to cry. Watching the ducks made me want to cry more. I felt like a little girl again and the painfully shy teenager, overflowing with sympathy and empathy for everything and everyone but mostly for animals. I remembered when I was fourteen and I had my first boyfriend, Jamie. We spent a lot of time out in the countryside as we both lived on the edges of the city. We walked in the fields, petted horses, sat in the shade of the leafy summer trees. It was all innocent, chatting, laughing, sometimes kissing.

One summer evening we were heading back home after such a walk when we ran into some of his school friends who were torturing a duck for fun. They were holding it over a fire. One held its head and the other its legs. Its neck was passed periodically through the flames. It was still alive for it emitted a pitiful quack as we witnessed its torture. The torturers were laughing, enjoying the power they held over this poor creature who could only suffer at their whim. Something snapped in me like a dry twig when I saw this scene. I screamed profanities and flew at them in an uncontrollable rage which burned higher and hotter than any fire they could make. I hit and spat and cried and was so filled with white hot and cold primordial anger that I wasn't even conscious of my actions. I don't remember making a decision to act. I just acted. I saw that wretched creature at the hands of those buffoons, those snarling, rabid, hillbilly scumbags and I wanted to tear the life out of them with my bare hands. I couldn't stop. Jamie was suddenly holding my arms. The morons had let the duck go, shocked and pale but trying to laugh. Thinking 'Oh you crazy bitch, it's only a fucking duck. You eat them, don't you? It's only food. It doesn't feel pain. It's too stupid. Lowlife.'

Like them.

Streams of words were coming from their mouths as if in a dream or a slow motion movie where the words don't match the mouths. Distorted and nightmarish. Everyone was black with charred firewood for one of them had fallen onto the fire and extinguished it with his big boots but not before he had fanned the flames with his flapping trouser legs and singed them to hell.

'Mummy, some crazy mental bitch attacked me today and pushed me into a camp fire just because we were roasting a duck alive.' Sunday chapel trousers ruined because some silly bitch went all sentimental over a dumb animal.

Dust and smoke and tears of rage stung my eyes. The morons became threatening once they had recovered from this unexpected attack from a small girl in a homemade skirt. Embarrassment made them more aggressive. Jamie led me away, shushing.

The duck lay on the grass. It was probably dead. It was difficult to tell. I hoped it was.

Sitting on the park bench had made me very cold. I got up, shivered and decided to go back to the flat. It seemed whilst this horror home video was playing in my head that I had come to a decision. I walked back to Rue MC Fouriérès in the fading light. My breath turning to steam in the pink, frosty light. The stars were coming out. It would be cold tomorrow, I thought. Winter was on the way.

I heard excited chatter as I put my key in the lock. Disjointed words fluttering loose from bouncing sentences and dancing together in the air of the small living room. M and Kristiana were seated on the sofa, a tray of tea and biscuits on the floor before them. Kristiana's cream pashmina had been tossed aside and lay carefully arranged over a chair so as to look carelessly abandoned, as if in a setting for a still life oil painting. M's cheeks were red and glowing with cold. They both looked windswept and were engrossed in their chatter. I was pale and half frozen by comparison, both in mood and countenance. At first they didn't notice me. The wind howled outside and the bald branches from the poplar tree outside tapped against the small window. A lumpy candle burned on the bedside table.

"It's exquisite," Kristiana purred, her voice like melting butter.

M was nodding frantically.

"Fantastic, what luck," she agreed, dunking a biscuit into her tea.

"Hi," I said. The deadpan syllable landed flatly amidst their bubbles of enthusiasm.

M looked up surprised to see me then grinned broadly her 'wicked pixie' grin. Her eyes dancing and catching the light from the candle reflecting it. She glanced sidelong at Kristiana who was smiling cat-like, cool and perfecting the art of looking bored.

"Shall we tell her Kris?" she asked.

Kris didn't answer. M looked at me sheepishly then grinned even more broadly.

"We've found a flat," she burst.

"A big spacious flat, cheap too, wooden floors, three bedrooms, two floors, bay windows, balcony Oh Charlotte it's fabulous, you'll love it, just wait till you see it," she went on, "it's perfect."

"Perfect," echoed Kristiana dreamily.

"Perfect," I thought, "my sister and Kristiana sharing a flat which neither of them could probably afford. Kristiana can glide around all day on the wooden floors, floating from room to room."

"We're putting down the deposit tomorrow morning, 1200 Francs," M carried on brushing crumbs from her lap, "Then 1200 Francs per month plus utilities and bla bla bla, it's a gift."

"I found the place purely by accident," Kristiana added with an air of waiting to be congratulated.

"What's wrong with this place M, I thought you liked it?" I asked taking off my coat and unwinding my scarf. I tossed them on top of Kristiana's 'still life pashmina arrangment'. She glanced quickly up as if my garments were contaminating hers.

"Oh," M said and there was a pause as if she were herself trying to think of a good enough reason to move into a huge flat with someone she hardly knew.

"It's time to move out of here, it's shabby and tired," she said at last.

Kristiana's words, shabby and tired. This was M, my sister who bought industrial sized bags of lentils at the market and who rolled cigarettes from the left over tobacco in the bottom of her pockets and shopped for second hand clothes. She didn't notice shabby and tired things, she quite liked them. Shabby and tired had character, personality, history. This was sailing girl's influence; Three bedrooms, polished floors, bay windows. This was her idea.

"Well I hope you can afford it," I said, holding back the speech I really wanted to give but not wanting to give Kristiana the satisfaction. M was all grown up. She could make up her own mind and if she got into debt or trouble then she would have to sort it out herself. This was exactly the difference between M and her new Swiss friend. M didn't have parents who could bail her out in a heartbeat with their platinum credit card.

I looked around the bed-sit.

"Well I like it here. It's kitsch and cosy.....and cheap."

Kristiana snorted. She tossed her hair and set her orange tea-cup on the tray.

"It's all a question of how you want to live, we can have a beautiful place for a little more each per month than M is paying for this dump. You should come and see it with us tomorrow. It's even got an old Reims style wrought iron balcony, a lovely feature."

'A lovely feature', I thought. Did she think she was at an architect's lunch trying to impress some of daddy's friends? Just the sort of thing a pashmina-wearing photography student would say. Phoney (even though I hate that awful American word it sort of suited her). Phoney, false, superficial and shallow.

"Awesome," she continued as if reading my mind and producing another awful American word to annoy me with.

"Yes come see it tomorrow, Charlotte," M coaxed, "then, you'll change your mind, you'll be green with envy."

I very much doubted that. I couldn't think of anything worse than sharing an interior designer's paradise with Kristiana and her spider eyes and the lurking ghost of daddy's Swiss bank account.

I mumbled a non-committal and headed for the kitchenette to make a fresh brew. The phone rang as the kettle boiled and M reached for her portable. She babbled breathlessly in French to the unseen caller and Kristiana mouthed at me, "It's Guy," and smiled her creamy smile. Oh lord, I thought, It's 'Jesus' on the phone and the sailing queen on the sofa. I think I'll go out and join the ducks in the park again.

Suddenly M slammed down the phone and jumped off the sofa as if she'd just been bitten in the arse.

"*Guy, Guy, mon amour, il vient chez nous ce soir, oh la la*.....it's Guy he's coming round tonight, he's says he's been thinking about me all day," she gushed, running headlong into her bedroom.

Kristiana and I exchanged bewildered looks and then continued in stilted small talk while M busied herself in anticipation of the 'coming of Jesus'. I felt suddenly relaxed despite Kristiana's presence. The events of the day and the cold autumn air had made me worn out and drowsy. The wind continued to howl outside and the bald poplar continued to tap rhythmically against the now steamed-up kitchen window. Stereolab beat out their heady, synthetic cadence in the background and sang. "*La lune est libre ce soir, la lune est libre je crois*". It was dark now but we couldn't see if the moon was free or not because of the thick blue clouds that hid her.

When M emerged from the bedroom she looked fresh and pretty and pixie-like. She was wearing a cherry-red, home-knit jumper with a rolled neck, grey slightly flared trousers and navy-blue Doc Martins. Her strawberry blond hair was twisted up into two stubby pigtails which gave the impression of small horns. Each pig tail was bound with lime green plastic bobbles which wobbled and caught the light of the candle. She even wore perfume. It was heavy, musky and herbal. Like clove oil and cinnamon.

"You look very nice," I said and meant it, "Is Guy coming for dinner?"

"I don't know," she replied, lighting a Gauloise and settling down on the chair in a miasma of smoke.

"No definite plans."

"Why don't we all go to L'Apostrophe for dinner? The brasserie there is lovely," Kristiana piped up.

M shrugged, her eyes dancing, the corners of her mouth twitching.

"Why not indeed?"

"Maybe I'll give it a miss," I said, "I have a lot to do tonight and besides, I spent half the afternoon in a café waiting for you."

M clapped her hand over her mouth and looked at Kristiana.

"Oh Charlotte, I'm so sorry I completely forgot about you what with the flat hunting and everything."

Kristiana looked blank then her glossed mobile mouth suddenly gaped into a perfect O shape.

"So we did, oh how could we, we got so carried away by the moment," she rushed.

"Oh it doesn't matter, I bumped into a few people from the *Fac* and Madame Guilloutine," I lied.

"We went for a coffee at Lafayette."

Madame Guilloutine was the landlady at the Glue pot, Welsh pub at the Place d'Erlan. She was unmistakably French, over fifty and still wearing killer stilettos and her black hair in a perfect chignon. Her name was not actually Guilloutine but Guillou and the pun was irresistible. We talked to her a lot when we went there. She was friendly and bubbly and didn't care whether you contributed to the conversation or not so long as she could talk. It seemed quite plausible that I should bump into her in town. It was a vague and easy lie.

"I can take care of myself when I'm stood up," I said and forced a convincing smile.

"Well we are sorry, aren't we Kris?" M said apologetically, "but come tonight and we'll have a nice meal and a few beers, I'll pay."

I was almost tempted but I had made up my mind in the park that day that I had to make a change and no more procrastination. I would do it. Tomorrow I would leave. No more sitting in lonely cafés waiting for M to drag herself away from her new found friends. No more hanging around on the edges of French conversations catching a few words and trying to fill in the rest. Besides I had to let her get on with her new life here. It was time to go and find mine.

"I have to pack," I said suddenly.

"Pack?" M asked raising her left eyebrow, "where are you going?"

"Amsterdam," I answered smiling naturally now as if this were indeed exactly where I should be going. "I'm going to Amsterdam."

II

That night the body dreams began. I was walking around an empty car park at night. I was looking for a large bin or a skip or just a dark and shadowy place to hide something. I was carrying something in a black plastic bin bag. It was very heavy and it smelled. It smelled like sulphur and rotting grapes and dog shit. It smelled rich, wet and fertile and ripe. In the dream I was desperate to rid myself of this burden. In the dream I had done something terrible but I was unsure just exactly what it was. I only knew I had to get rid of whatever was in this sack. I had to physically unburden myself then I knew that I would feel relieved; that I would be exonerated, forgiven; that I would be wiped clean. As I walked around the car park I began to feel more and more that there was nowhere I could put this, this thing, whatever it was in the sack. And I couldn't just put it down. I had to hide it. It was becoming more and more urgent that I hide it and run. And then it became apparent in the dream what I was carrying in the sack.

It was the torso of a man.

The alarm clock went off suddenly like a siren, invading my very soul, shaking me out of the shadowy nightmare where my sub consciousness tortured itself. I woke immediately, relieved, released from the hellish world of dark car parks and body parts. I re emerged slowly into the world of reality. I was going to Amsterdam today to begin my new life. I shuddered with fear and anticipation. I felt a mixture of terror and exhilaration. I dragged myself up out of my warm nest and into the cold bathroom. I had a lot to do. As well as booking my train ticket I had to call ahead to a few hostels and the employment agency, which I had been putting off until now. A few hospitals in Amsterdam were looking for nursing staff and I had a good chance of getting a job there and though it seemed slightly less glamorous than teaching (but only slightly), at least it was something I could do alone and it was a start.

I passed the day making the necessary calls, packing and tidying up M's place. It went very fast and all too soon it was time to catch the train. M had come home around six.

"I'm off then," I called to her, feeling rather choked. I swallowed a lump in my throat.

No answer.

I set down my bags to go and find her.

"What are you doing?" I asked, feeling rather cross that she was ignoring me once again.

I crossed the small living room-kitchenette and spied her leaning out of the window into the chilly evening air.

"Looking at the stars," she said not turning to see me.

I smiled for it was our favourite Oscar Wilde quote.

"We are all in the gutter..." I began

"....but some of us are looking at the stars," she finished.

I came up behind her and squeezed her.

"See you in Holland then," I said, "you will come up North and visit when I get settled."

"Of course", she said and squeezed my hand.

"Do you think we become stars when we die?" she asked wistfully.

"I mean our bodies go back into the earth that is obvious but our minds, our mental energy, where does it go, it doesn't just disappear, it must get recycled too....into stars, I mean there are millions and trillions of them so why not?"

"It's not such a wild theory," I said, "and I guess we'll find out some day, until then may we carry on this great adventure that is life until death and may we always have the luck of the Irish…."

"…and the arrogance of the French," she finished, laughing.

She came in from the window and kissed me three times, which is the Northern French tradition. Her cheek was papery and ice cold against mine which was warmed through with nervous anticipation of my journey and beyond.

Chapter 6 – Amsterdam

I was sitting in my tiny bed-sit at the Vrije Universiteit Ziekenhuis, Amsterdam, Free University hospital or the *VU* as it was more affectionately known. I was surrounded by a vulgar mauve, the colour of dried blood. How appropriate for a hospital, I thought, amused. I watched the steady rain beat against the window. Listening to the sound made me drowsy. I yawned. I was so tired. I had never been so tired in my life. I hadn't been sleeping well and had been doing shift work as a nurses' assistant at the hospital, sometimes starting at 7:30 a.m. sometimes finishing at 11:00 p.m. Running across the courtyard that stretched between the staff quarters and the main hospital building in my white tunic, white trousers and white running shoes, enveloped in a luminous yellow plastic rain cape and hood, my head down against the wind, plastic flapping and the pitch black sky above, I must have looked like a member of a disaster plan crew who had deserted from a nuclear power plant meltdown.

It had been, in the end, very easy to get a job at the VU. I had spent the first few nights in a hostel in Amsterdam's colourful Warmoestraat close to the Red Light District and immediately visited the employment agency whose number I had brought with me from Ireland all those months ago, just in case I didn't get a job a the *Fac* in Reims. Luckily they were still recruiting and seven days later I was installed in my own room with a full-time three month contract. But now I was exhausted.

I yawned again and my jaw cracked. It was my day off, Wednesday. I was also free tomorrow. I had to shop, clean, do laundry, study Dutch and write letters. It felt like way too much energy expenditure. I also had to phone M. But I lay on my bed watching the rain, too tired to move.

I had been at the VU for two weeks. I had mixed feelings about it. Some days I felt small and embarrassed, stupid and harassed. Some days I was close to tears. Some days I hated the Dutch and their ridiculous little crowded puddle of a country. I hated their rudeness, their confidence, their coldness and their tallness.

But some days, especially during the morning coffee breaks where we sat down to drink coffee and eat *beskuitjes* (semi-sweet biscuits), when the team were friendly and I was able to follow little bits of the conversation and when the watery winter sun was trickling in through the dirty windows of the *koffie kamer*. I felt weary and peaceful and happy, like an overworked, drowsy farm animal, chewing contentedly. Of course I missed M and Taru and Angéline, even Guy, Etienne and Rémy in a strange way. And I missed Belfast, my friends there, my ordinary, safe, life there. I missed getting up in the morning and knowing exactly what to expect. But I didn't want it back. I had learned a lot about myself in the past few weeks alone and especially, that I was now a different person from the one who had boarded that flight to France some months ago. Long ago in another life.

I had always romantically seen myself as a flaming sunflower in a field of magnolias at home in Ireland. Parochial, suffocating, constricting Ireland. But here I was in another country, a foreigner, a misfit, a *buitenlander*. I was still a sunflower but now surrounded by not only magnolias, but orange lilies, violets, daisies and stinging nettles. Somehow it was like fitting in because no-one else did either.

Despite my physical tiredness and aching feet from the endless traipsing up and down the polished, ice-coloured corridors of the VU. And, despite my backache from the endless pushing of patients along the corridors in their beds to x-rays and barium tests and for MRI scans, them lying like stoic captains in great rolling ships, white sheets billowing like sails, I had that nice warm feeling that I was achieving something. I felt I had accomplished something difficult, cleared some hurdles and although there were many more to come, I had gotten this far. I had faced everything head on, not bottled out, not sat at home and wished I had the courage to leave but been too scared. I was rather proud of myself.

I finally dragged myself into a sitting position and got up. I shuffled along the blood-red corridor to the pay phone. It was situated in a corner to the left of the dank, overworked kitchen. It hung high up on the wall and I had to launch myself on to the high bar stool in front of it to be able to reach. Built for the Dutch, I thought. I rang M on her portable. She answered immediately and was excited to hear from me. After some exuberant spiel over Guy she said she could come up for a visit during my next days off which were the following Thursday and Friday.

"Oh!" she cried suddenly just as we were about to hang up.

"Can I bring Angéline and Taru?"

"Of course," I answered at once, pleased and already looking forward to seeing them all, "as long as they don't mind sleeping on the floor, bring bags."

"*D'accord*", M replied, her Northern Irish accent making her *R* sound much too harsh for the soft French word. "*Parfait, à bientôt ma petite soeur.*"

"*Goed zo, tot straks mijn klein zusje.*" I replied in my best, newly acquired Dutch, hoping indeed to see her soon. My harsh *R* came in very useful for this more guttural language.

She giggled.

We hung up. The nurses' rooms were deadly silent except for the steady beat of rain on the glass. Lashing, as my mother would have said. We have lots of different words for rain in Ireland, I suppose, in the same way the Scandinavians have lots of different words for snow (or is that a myth?) Ranging, in level of severity from, bucketing, lashing and teeming to *skiffling* and spitting then there was the type of rain you couldn't see or hear, but which completely soaked you as soon as you walked outdoors. Like a heavy mist.

Despite the weather, I really had to get out of my little, blood-red cave otherwise I'd go insane. I needed to explore a little. So far I'd spent my evenings and free days (after the chores and study) in Sinieke's room down the hall. Sinieke was a middle-aged theatre nurse who offered me bitter coffee and sweet tales of her many travels in Asia, Africa and America. She sat tall and gaunt and unmarried in her high wicker chair from Thailand and her eyes flashed with the memory of her adventures.

Some evenings I'd go for a beer with her or with Saskia, a dark-eyed Polish girl who was especially sweet and relaxing company. We'd sit in dim candle-lit cafés discussing love and life and the Dutch till way after midnight. We'd press our fingertips into the soft white candle wax or make little dips in the side where the melted wax which had formed a pool around the wick, could escape and run down the sides in rivulets and harden before reaching the bottom. It looked like the walls of an ancient ice cave. I liked Saskia because she reminded me of M when M was being nice.

I went back to my room, grabbed my raincoat and bag and went out into the deluge.

I had made many observations of the Dutch since arriving here three weeks ago and, whilst being aware that Amsterdam was not a true representation of the Netherlands' culture in much the same way as Dublin is not a true representation of the Irish culture, I had observed two distinctive types of '*Amsterdammer*'. There were, in the first instance the well-heeled, affluent, conservative types who work in banks and corporations, who sip tall glasses of chilled white wine in cafés on late Sunday mornings whilst reading the broadsheet newspapers and smoking rough tobacco. The man's hair would be a little too long, making him look scruffy compared to his British counterpart and, more often than not, he sports an unruly moustache. The woman meanwhile, would be predominantly bottle or enhanced blond but sometimes boast a shock of bright red or slightly orange spiked and tussled hair which would not look out of place on a twenty-something art student but which is here, in Amsterdam, perfectly acceptable and approved of. She would usually be prematurely aged, having spent too much time on the sun bed or soaking up the summer rays which come more frequently and strongly in Holland than in Ireland. Although the winters were much the same, the Dutch summers were by far, dryer and sunnier. She would typically have high cheekbones and slightly up-tilted eyes giving her, perhaps undeservedly, a haughty look. And despite being 1.80 metres in height, she would wear high-heeled boots which click neatly on the cobbled street the cadence of wealth, of browsing in antique shops and of sipping espresso on a sunny terrace.

In the second instance there were the less conventional types. The people who were drawn to Amsterdam because of its tolerance and its liberalism and its spirit of freedom. They were both young and old. They were students of philosophy, art, science, literature and of life. They were Rastafarians, hippies, anarchists, punks, poets, musicians and actors. They were advocates of animal rights, of human rights, gay rights, freedom of thought, speech, dress and expression. They were campaigners for the environment, for political change and social change. They were the rejecters of capitalism, consumerism, globalisation, corporations, monopolisation and privatisation. They were the absinthe drinkers of their own time, the dabblers in soft drugs, the talkers and the dreamers. They were Amsterdam in its ceremonial robes.

I loved the city in its noise and business and colour. The bicycles whizzed past alongside trams, taxis and cars. Crossing the road was perilous. I was amazed at the array of bicycles. Many were customised both as a theft deterrent and as a form of self-expression. I saw leopard-print bicycles, green furry upholstered bicycles, one with plastic flowers wound around the frame and handlebars, one with paper streamers wrapped around now sticking to the frame in a mushy pulp in the rain, luminous yellow ones, indigo, lilac, orange, shocking pink, striped red and white like a Barbour's pole and some which looked like they'd been spray painted by a two-year-old child; paint everywhere even on the wheels and seat. I even saw a turquoise tricycle which reminded me of one my father had assembled for me when I was about seven, from bits of 'dead' bicycles he had found in skips and lying prostrate and abandoned at roadsides. A Frankenstein tricycle.

Chapter 7 – *La Haye, la-haut*[5]

I

M and her entourage arrived the following Thursday around three. I was so excited all day I could hardly keep still. I only wished I had more friends for her to meet like she had in Reims, as a sign of my having settled in. I cleaned my little room, vacuumed the blood-red carpet and shopped for fresh coffee (a must when entertaining the French), red wine, fresh pasta, red pesto and some vegetables. Now I had the makings of a nice, easy meal whenever it was required.

We had arranged to meet in Het Hoekje, a small pub close to the station but not close enough to be an overpriced tourist trap and also minus the surly service.

I dashed in at ten past having been reprimanded by M for being 'too on time', on frequent occasions.

They were there already at a corner table. M was talking loudly in French and waving a cigarette. Taru sat smiling while she nursed a cup of chocolate and cream. Angéline sat wrapped in hat, coat and scarf looking around like a frightened rabbit.

Taru looked up first and waved. M leapt up and leaned across the table to do the greetings, scattering a thankfully empty coffee cup and drawing undesired attention to our meeting. We all exchanged the three cheek kisses which are

---

5. *La Haye, la-haut* - The Hague, up yonder

conveniently the same number in Holland as in the north of France.

Angéline sat down shivering.

"*Oh, il fait si froid*", she murmured, trying to smile through chattering teeth.

M rolled her eyes, "It's not the North pole, *ma pêche*, only Holland," she laughed.

M called Angéline 'my peach' when she was mothering her.

"Well it is pretty dreadful," I agreed, looking outside at the cold wet streets of Amsterdam. Sheets of rain and wet snow were sweeping through the narrow alleys in angry gusts. The sky was dark grey and it hadn't gotten quite light all day.

"Mmmm, November in Northern Europe, I love it," I said gazing out dreamily, half wishing to tease Angéline and half meaning it.

There *was* something delicious about winter. The darkness, the candlelight and the storms. It made me think of romantic, gothic stories where wind-swept heroes and heroines fling their exhausted, rain drenched bodies from high cliffs and into black toiling seas, their hearts broken, their passions too great for this mortal world.

This was passionate weather. The gods were angry.

Angéline's dark French eyes widened in surprise and we laughed. We ordered more coffee and hot chocolate. The waiter answered my bad Dutch with good English. Taru ordered a slice of strawberry tart and sat contemplating in for a long time before eating it.

"But it looks so beautiful," she sighed taking her first reluctant bite.

After the second round of drinks we settled the bill and set off for the VU and my humble abode. I had reckoned on cooking the pasta tonight and opening a few bottles of red. The girls had no objections; even M went along with the plan.

"What should we do tomorrow?" I asked as we ran across the road to the number five tram to Amstelveen. I had to shout to be heard over the wind and my coat flapped wildly around me.

"Lets go to the beach," yelled M who was behind me, holding firmly on to Angéline and steering her by the elbow in the right direction.

"Are you nuts? In this weather?" I shouted back.

"Especially in this weather. The sea will be glorious," M answered as we reached the tram and boarded relieved, dripping and out of breath. M's cheeks looked like red apples and her left eyebrow was raised expectantly.

"Well, we'll see how it goes tomorrow," I said diplomatically. This storm had been raging for days and it was likely it would rage tomorrow too.

"If it's not especially bad, we could go to the beach," I said lowering my voice in case Angéline overheard. I was secretly banking on the continuing storm. I didn't really have the energy to train it to Den Haag where the best beaches are. I looked behind us where Taru and Angéline sat chatting in French, Angéline oblivious to the fact that we were plotting to spend a day at the beach, up here, in November, in the rain. I smiled at them not having the heart to divulge our plans, at least not until they were definite.

II

I awoke the next day, stiff from spending the night on the floor in a sleeping bag but nonetheless, refreshed. I had given M my bed for one night. I opened my eyes and noticed immediately that the wind had stopped. The storm was noticeable by its absence. It was calm.

'Shit!' I thought.

There was even a feeble glimmer of light in the sky beyond the curtains. It wouldn't pass for sun normally but today, compared with the previous week's impenetrable cloud cover, it would do.

'Yes you shall go to the ball Cinderella,' I thought, M gets her way again.

Suddenly the bathroom door opened with its usual creak and Taru emerged, showered and fresh.

"So shall we go to La Haye?" she asked, rubbing her head vigorously with a turquoise towel.

"It was a surprise...but actually..." I rolled over on to my knees then stood up tentatively, walked the two steps required to reach the window and peered out through the maroon curtain, "it's not at all a bad day. Could work."

M stirred from the bed and squinted at us.

"The sea, yippee, we're going to see the sea," she cried. She leaned down to shake Angéline who was asleep on the floor right next to the bed.

"*Ma pêche, nous allons à la plage aujourd'hui, alors, maintenant.*"

There was no reply. Only a faint rustle of nylon as ma pêche tunneled deeper into her nest.

Taru put her finger to her lips to shut M up.

"*Elle a peur de la mer en hiver,*" she whispered, wide-eyed.

M tutted and reached to the bed side table for her tobacco, papers and lighter. As if anyone could be scared of the sea in winter or at any time, her face said.

"It's OK ma pêche, we are going south," she teased. M swung her legs out of the bed and sat on the edge. She was wearing a long red T-shirt which did not cover her knees. Her legs were the colour of lilac marble and the polished ice of the hospital floors.

We drank coffee and took the tram to Centraal Station where we caught the train to Den Haag. From there we could easily get a tram to Scheveningen beach. Angéline sat in silence throughout the journey looking out the window at the speeding, flat, contrived countryside with her large brown eyes.

When we disembarked, I realised I had made a mistake by assuming that the weather would be the same as it was sixty kilometres north in Amsterdam. Being Irish I should have known a short distance can make a complete difference, especially in a small country with a sea climate. The storm was still raging in Den Haag and it was positively livid at the coast in Scheveningen.

As the North Sea battered the coast, the scene was terrific. The sea was brown, grey and muddy blue. The crashing waves whipped up a froth of dirty lace foam spray which blew up the beach and on to the promenade like a possessed cappuccino.

The sea rolled, tossed and thrashed like a wild, suffering beast. The sand was hard, brown and sugary underfoot like wet fudge. Farther away from the sea where the sand was drier, the wind whipped it up and flung it into our faces. Nostrils, eyes and mouths were flayed with the finest and palest of ground glass. M screamed in delight opening wide her arms as if to catch the wind and sail off in it. Angéline screamed but for different reasons. We only stayed a few more minutes then I took charge and we stumbled back to the promenade like four Lawrences of Arabia in a sandstorm. M had had her sea.

We took the tram back into the town centre to warm up and pacify the traumatised Angéline. Her face was as pale as a sheet of ice in contrast to her dark hair that hung in damp salty tails. I asked everyone what they wanted to do and Angéline suggested an art museum. It seemed like a very good idea to be indoors, warm and looking at old paintings after M's madness which had gotten us all thoroughly cold and damp. So we went to the Mauitshuis museum to see some dreary Rembrandts and not so dreary Vermeers. Angéline thawed out and came to life in the museum. It was quiet and calming the way museums and libraries are. You feel the need to tread softly and to whisper as if the people in the portraits are real and listening to your every word.

That night, as we all lay in the twilight between wakefulness and sleep (Angéline had the honour of the bed to make up for having been subjected to the beach), I suddenly remembered the unicorn.

I sat up in my sleeping bag.

"M," I called softly, "are you awake?"

"Mmmm," she murmured groggily.

"I forgot to ask you about the unicorn. I noticed it was missing. Is it lost?"

There was a momentary silence. Then a faint stirring.

"M?" I asked again.

"I don't know actually, maybe someone broke it and hid the evidence," she answered at last.

I felt cross with her for being so nonchalant and careless about our lovely talisman.

It felt personal.

"How can you not know what happened? Didn't you ask people who'd visited if they knocked it over or took it?" I said, irritation creeping into my voice.

There came a tut in the darkness.

"Who would steal it?" she asked indignantly, as if she herself had been accused of the very act. As if accusing her friends was tantamount to accusing her.

I thought suddenly of her plans to move in with Kristiana. Mentioning theft made me immediately visualize the floating, beatific Kristiana.

Silence again.

"Maybe you'll find it when you are packing for your move," I said sighing and lying back again not wishing to be further irritated by her at this late hour.

A longer silence ensued. There came a gentle snore from Taru.

"Actually that's all off," M replied finally.

I was delighted and couldn't help a broad grin from spreading across my face. I was glad it was dark and she couldn't see me.

"Oh? How come?" I asked trying to sound matter of fact.

A sigh. The soft gurgle of a waste pipe somewhere in the building.

"Oh it was way too expensive and besides, Kris decided she needed to be in Paris this year for her studies you know... and I need to save up too, maybe travel more this year or start a study somewhere, another country," she replied.

"Good, I'm glad, it would have been a mistake."

I was still grinning and trying to keep the 'I told you so' tone from my voice.

"C'est la vie," M murmured, "I'll have a good look for the unicorn when I get back, maybe it dropped off the shelf."

"I'm dropping off," I said yawning, "somehow the sound of voices in the dark when I'm all cosy makes me feel all safe and sleepy."

"Like being read a story," M said and she too, yawned.

"Exactly like that," I answered, "anyway, *bonne nuit, welterusten* and nighty night"

I turned over on my side where I would sleep until the hard floor dug into my hip so much that it would wake me up.

"Exactly," I thought. M hit the nail on the head then. I hadn't had a story read to me for a long time. But the memory of it was still strong enough to invoke those feelings of childlike security, warmth and sleep. Mummy's voice reading stories about animals and enchanted forests, princesses, magical kingdoms and brave knights. Me, enveloped in fuzzy blankets, wide-eyed, anticipating the end but fighting sleep and usually losing the battle. Sometimes feeling scared at the exciting bits but still safe. Feeling a kind of second hand fear and knowing I was safely tucked up and protected. Still, today, listening to someone's voice reading and the rustle of turning pages makes me immediately drowsy.

But some nights ended in tears. Some nights mummy read a book called *A Home for Whiskers*. The first time she read it I burst into tears at the end and was inconsolable. I sobbed myself to sleep. Salty tears burned my cheeks and soaked the white pillow case. I blew bubbles of snot from the end of my nose where they burst in a sticky spray.

"But Whiskers finds a home in the end," mummy would cajole, "he's happy now."

Whiskers was a tabby kitten with white feet and breast. He was lost in the woods and couldn't find anywhere to live. He was hungry and alone. He came across a snail and asked if he could go home with the snail. Mr. Snail laughed and said his home was on his back and there certainly wasn't room enough for Whiskers too. Next he met an otter and asked if he could go home with him. Mr. Otter laughed too and swam across the river to his watery den leaving poor Whiskers behind on the bank. He met other creatures (which I no longer remember), who all in turn laughed at poor Whiskers and went to their respective homes without him.

In the end Whiskers met a little girl whose father was chopping wood in the forest. I can still remember the illustration on this particular page. She has blond plaits and is wearing a red gingham dress and she bends down to pat Whiskers. The she picks him up and takes him home with her.

A happy ending indeed. But I still cried. I persuaded mummy to read it again and again. Each time promising I wouldn't cry. Each time logically and coherently (as a five year old can be) discussing with her the ending and the fact that Whiskers got a nice home. And each time, I cried. I lay there biting my lip to stop it wobbling, breaths coming in short gasps, chest heaving, eyes filling, holding it back. But the dam burst and mummy would tuck me up crossly, tutting and vowing to throw away the book.

But she never did.

III

The next day was Friday. We were all tired and traipsed around the shops in a kind of daze. Taru and Angéline decided to go back to France in the evening. M was going to stay on for the weekend and was persistently persuading me to call in sick at the VU. I very was tempted. The storm was over, the sun shone, weakly but was present nevertheless and the prospect of hiring bicycles and visiting a town, somewhere pretty like Delft was very tempting. But I hadn't decided. I still had obligations. Still, Delft was reputedly very charming. I stepped outside the large Kruidvat chemist shop as the girls were taking such a long time buying shampoo and *disques* which Angéline insisted upon and which no Dutch shop assistant had ever heard of. (They turned out to be make-up removal pads). Angéline never wore make-up and I wondered why she wanted them.

I stood outside for what seemed like an hour. I smoked a cigarette. I walked up, walked down, looked at my watch again. Finally M, Taru and Angéline emerged from the shop.

"*Merde*," said M immediately, "I feel sick."

"*Moi aussi*," chimed in the other two in agreement.

Sick? Why sick? I thought, then M took my arm and steered me hastily away from the chemist's.

Taru began her rant as we ambled along the crowded pavement, "Dis, dis outrageous consumerism," she began.

"I see twenty-five, no, forty different kinds of shampoo, dry hair, fat hair, thin hair, normal, for grey, for blond with Chinese herbs, against frizz, straightening shampoo, colour shampoo, with banana with kiwi fruit with lemon, mousse for 'surf look' hair whatever it is, wet-look gel...oh la la I don't know whether to eat it or wash my hair with it..." she breathed deeply as if truly nauseated by the whole sickening display.

M was nodding appreciatively. Taru carried on, now gaining momentum.

"When I lived in east Germany," she continued. "There were two maybe three types of shampoo, one toothpaste, no body scrubs, no eye lash curlers and we lived perfectly good without them."

"And you know what?" M added fishing a careworn rolled-up cigarette from the pocket of her leather jacket, "I like the sound of that much better. You go in, you buy the shampoo and you leave. No stress. No standing fixated before the nauseating array of garbage."

"Who needs all that choice? And who are the people who produce it? Who thinks we need all that shit?"

Taru was nodding furiously, "It's the same with everything, everywhere you go, fifty brands of *douche* gel, twenty types of tampons."

Angéline giggled.

But M continued vehemently,

"And new products flooding the market every week to tempt us to buy them. New products we don't need, products dripped into little rabbit's eyes and rubbed into the skin of cats, dogs and monkeys, just to make a new product. Just to produce more bloody rubbish no one needs that will sit around someone's bathroom cabinet for a decade and then be discarded in its plastic bottle to lie around in landfill for the next thousand years as a testimony to the frivolity and shallowness of human nature. I find it so disgusting that I am standing in front of all this nonsense and wasted money and resources and some animal is dying of pain and misery in a metal cage so I can have another hair colouring and some people in the world cannot get enough food to eat today never mind buying a new hair product...I mean isn't it all wrong? Fundamentally really wrong?"

I nodded. "The massive suffering of many to provide a limited luxury to a few. Kind of the opposite to utilitarianism."

We were all deep in serious thought now, even Angéline who had followed little of the conversation, I guessed, was frowning intensely so I suggested going in for tea to calm everyone down.

"Which sort of tea?" Taru asked, "Chamomile, ginger, Indian, Chinese? Tea to make you sleepy, tea to wake you up?"

I pushed her gently.

"Don't get stressed Taru," I said smiling, "and I promise I won't take you shopping again."

She managed a grimace and we went in for tea. Well, a half-filled cup of tepid water followed half an hour later by a teabag presented in a grand wooden box.

Taru wanted to go back to Reims because she had promised to take care of her grandmother for the weekend while her mother went to visit friends in Charleville. Angéline wanted to go because...she just wanted to go home. She was one of the French who felt like a fish out of water, out of France.

Taru sipped her tepid strawberry flavoured tea then suddenly clamped her hand over her mouth as if remembering something vital.

"I forgot to unlock my flip flop," she cried.

Tea sprayed in a projectile jet from M's mouth as she almost choked and then rejected the liquid in the nick of time. She doubled up with laughter. I too was convulsing with my hand over my mouth, brown liquid seeping out from the corners, tears of mirth filling my eyes. Angéline looked at us as if we were mad.

"What the hell are you talking about?" M managed after a few minutes snorting and sniffling into a kind of composure.

"How do you unlock a flip flop?"

That set us all off again.

"Oh la la!" Taru said shaking her head, "I don't know how I am so funny."

Then Angéline surprised everyone by chirping up.

"For her cat," she said, looking at us as if we were all completely stupid.

"The cat, Fou-fou, he goes in and out through the flip flop, a *chatière*, a little door for cats"

The penny dropped and M and I looked at each other in disbelief.

"She means a cat flap", M squealed delighted by this new linguistic mishap.

"Oh I must write this one down"

Taru smiled wanly and flipped a soggy beer mat across the table catching M between the eyes. She waved a finger at me.

"And you," she said pretending to be angry but starting to laugh.

"I forgot to lock my CAT flop and Fou fou will be outside and in all the day with friends and boyfriends coming in and out."

We stifled further giggles and M wiped her eyes.

"You are a linguist's dream," M said smiling.

And suddenly we had forgotten about the stress in the chemist shop.

Chapter 8 – Delft

I was pedalling away on a cycle path of red brick heading south from Den Haag to Delft. M was ahead of me, headphones on, a large joint between her lips. She was listening to the loud hypnotic techno thud of Laurent Garnier and couldn't hear me shouting directions.

I had followed her mischievous advice and called in sick at the hospital. I didn't feel good about it, but it was done and I was determined to enjoy the day with my sister. We had taken a train to Den Haag again as it was within cycling distance to the charming city of Delft where M was insistent about going, and hired bicycles at the station. But I was irritated and tired. M was being a pain, insisting on smoking hash on the way and ignoring my warning shouts about traffic. And I had had the body dream again last night.

This time I was at my parent's house in Belfast in what used to be my room or the 'box room' as it was endearingly called because of its size. But there was a terrible smell in the room and I could not sleep. I got up in my long, nylon, ladybird-patterned nightgown (for I was young in the dream, six or seven). I followed the smell and it seemed to be coming from the wall behind the bed. I sank down in the gap between the wall and the bed on my child's knees and began to investigate. The wall paper was coming off in one corner so I began to pick at it...pick, pick, pick,...how I loved to pick at peeling paper when I was a child and this was more exciting because not only was the paper coming off but the plaster underneath was loose too. I gasped and swept my hair out of my eyes as it was long then, long and fine and golden blond. I dug with my tiny white paws at the plaster and it began falling to the floor in large damp, chalky chunks, the smell getting stronger.

I gagged at the sulphurous, rotting, cloying stench. I tried holding my breath, then breathing only through my mouth. Then I recoiled in the utmost horror as I drew back to admire my handiwork. There lay the dismembered body of M, chopped up into bits and stuffed into the wall cavity behind my bed. She was recognisable only by her eyes which stared out at me - dead fish eyes in a sea of brick. I whimpered and suddenly started clawing at the mound of plaster on the floor. I had to get it back I had to cover it up. Oh why oh why had I looked? I was overwhelmed with guilt and shame. It was me, in the child's dream; I had done this deed and had somehow forgotten. Now I remembered and I was frantic to re-hide the evidence. I stuffed chunks of damp plaster back into the cavity to cover M's white, corpse-face.

I had awakened to enormous relief and to the sound of M grinding her teeth in her sleep as she lay on the floor in her sleeping bag.

Now I was cycling wildly to keep up with her and she was so full of energy and carried away that I could hardly manage it. There was a headwind and I was breathless. The old bicycles we'd hired were more for endurance than speed. My legs were like lead. Just up ahead there was some sort of crossing for trams and I sighed with relief at the prospect of stopping for a few minutes. If I could catch up with M, I could persuade her to stop and we could drink the cola that was swishing around in my rucksack. But M was apparently oblivious to the oncoming tram. The hundred ton, butterscotch cream and dark red of the *Haagsche* (from Den Haag) tram was trundling right for us and she didn't seem to see it. Of course she didn't hear it, what with Laurent Garnier booming in her ears. I suddenly began to panic. I pedalled furiously with the last of my strength to catch her and stop her. I was so close I could see the dark pink of the back of her ears and where her blond hair, damp with sweat was pasted to the back of her neck. I shouted but to no avail above the music and the wind. My voice sounded shrill and out of control. I looked around to see if there was anyone ahead I could hail to stop her. There was no one. A few Fresian cows lifted their heavy heads to examine the scene then resumed eating grass, unconcerned. The tram trundled on seeming faster now. I felt I was caught in one of my nightmares. The crossing where the tram tracks traversed the cycle path glinted in the bright sun like evil teeth. The illuminated bicycle light signal that is commonplace in Holland as well as traffic lights for cars was red. Stop.

"Stop," I thought, "she must stop."

M was almost on the tram track. I screamed one final ditched attempt to slow her.

"M!" I yelled, my voice breaking with the effort.

My head was filled with thoughts. One chasing another. 'She can't stop. She's going too fast. The tram can't stop. It's going too fast. It can't avoid her. It can't swerve. She *still* doesn't see it. She's going to be killed.'

I was filled with panic and dread and helplessness. M was going to be killed and I couldn't stop it. I would have to watch it.

What would I do without her? That last thought was inconceivable. I shut my eyes to shut it out. To shut out the scene which gathered momentum before me and was rushing to a final point over which I had no control.

Suddenly I heard the screech of breaks and the roar of the tram passing by us. So close I felt the warm air from its engine like the breath of some exhausted beast. I smelt the burning metal of wheels on tracks.

But there was no crash. No horn sounded. No bell.

I opened my eyes.

M had stopped in the nick of time. She stood astride her black *omafiets* (granny bicycle) and stared at the passing vehicle. She turned to me and took off her headset, grinning.

'Where did that come from?" she asked, sounding surprised.

I dismounted my bicycle and collapsed on the grass verge by the path. I let my bike fall jingling and clanking to the soft ground. I lay like that for some time looking up at the sky and the sheep clouds hurrying by in the wind.

"You were almost flattened," I said to her at last.

M sniffed. She was sitting cross-legged beside me rolling a cigarette. She wrinkled her nose and shook her head.

"Nah," she said thoughtfully, "it wasn't my day to die."

"Well, I almost died of fright," I said in a monotone. I was just too tired now to get angry or excited. I felt drained. The after effects of adrenalin rush, I supposed.

I closed my eyes.

"Make me a cigarette," I said, "it's the least you can do after giving me a fright like that."

M humphed and fished in her pouch for some remnants of tobacco.

Anyway I was too relieved to nag her about it. A near miss is as good as a mile our dad would have said and it's true.

As M rolled me a cigarette I thought of a funny story her friend Alex had told one night in a clammy pub in Dublin a few years back.

They had been in Germany studying together and had met up in Berlin at the weekend. Alex was, as usual, broke and suffered, as a passionate smoker, more harshly. He had immediately asked M to make him a cigarette as soon as they met and she had humphed very much as she had done just now with me but, reluctantly, fished in the mouldy depths of her pocket for some shrivelled tobacco shreds which were dried-up and mixed with the residue of various other pocket artefacts, and proceeded to make for Alex what, in principle, was a cigarette.

The finished item was passed proudly to him. His profuse gratitude was accepted without comment and he began leisurely to smoke it. Then M proceeded to open her bag and take out a brand new, shining plastic envelope of fat and bulging Drum tobacco. She opened it, took some of the moist and sweet smelling shreds, placed it on a fresh white paper and made herself a beautiful, fresh cigarette. Alex was speechless but being sweet-natured, passed the incident off without reproach but retold it with much gusto one alcohol fuelled evening much to everyone's (even M's) amusement.

We lunched in Delft on the old town square in the shadow of the clock tower and ornate town hall with its cherry red wooden shutters and gold leaf lettering. It felt like being back in time, in the 14th or 15th century, except for the flapping yellow parasols emblazoned with adverts for Lipton's ice tea and Grolshe beer. Cobblestones underfoot and great brass church bells ringing out for something or other. It was quite warm for November, trapped in the sunny square and people were already on the terraces. This is what I really love about Europe. Eating and drinking on terraces. Even in temperatures of below ten degrees, the Europeans are out there, wrapped up in fur-trimmed anoraks, wearing sunglasses, drinking tiny cups of coffee with their gloves still on. They take every opportunity to soak up the winter sun and the atmosphere. In Belfast, people sit huddled indoors at plastic-topped tables even if it's warm outdoors. In Belfast no-one eats lunch on the pavement.

M and I chose a table outside next to the window. From my experiences in Holland so far, though they were not many, it was always a good idea to sit where you cannot easily be ignored. For one thing that Dutch waiters love to do is to try not to see you. They will make eye contact, but as if the eyes are somehow through you or behind you. They will do their utmost not to see you, not to hear you. I heard a story once from a Canadian who had just arrived in Holland and could not believe how they could ignore him so completely. There he sat calling once, twice then beckoning and finally waving to the waiter. Finally after twenty minutes or so, being completely fed up he stood up, waved and shouted loudly asking for his coffee, "May I please order a coffee?" Thereupon the waiter marched over put out his hand as if to redress the Canadian back into his seat and clipped briskly "*momentje*", before turning and marching off behind the bar. Shocked enough as the Canadian was, he could not believe his eyes as the waiter took from beneath the counter a squished pack of Marlboros and proceeded to light one in full view of the customers.

But ironically for M and me as soon as we sat down a young girl came over, smiled pleasantly and took our order for pancakes and coffee.

The pancakes came hot and greasy and with syrup and powder sugar. It was very sweet and messy but just what we needed after our long cycle and my fright. After lunch we sat soaking up the sun. I had sunglasses with me but M sat squinting into the light looking very childlike.

"How is Guy?"

M humphed and shrugged. "I am too busy to have a boyfriend at the moment,"

"You mean he's dumped you?" I teased.

She tutted and shook her head.

"No, I mean, I'm just too busy and I like being single and having lots of time alone and my own space and freedom, you know."

I nodded slowly. I was just beginning to realise how that can feel when you relax and enjoy it. When you don't have to worry about someone else. When you can watch awful TV in bed, have a sandwich instead of cooking dinner every day or change your plans at the last minute.

"I've started painting again and writing stories, as well as all my class preparations and social life I don't really have time for a relationship... and besides, he was getting clingy," she said rolling a cigarette.

"Too young," I answered thoughtfully, "probably looking for a mother figure."

M laughed heartily. Guy was only nineteen. It was probably for the best that M didn't have to look after him as well as herself.

"But life is good," she continued leaning back in the worn wicker chair and blowing smoke rings into the air, "and for you?"

I reflected a moment on past four months. It had been good and bad. Sometimes it had been awful, the loneliness, the getting used to a new job, new people, the embarrassment of making mistakes, missing my friends in Belfast, missing the warmth and security and familiarity of home but I would have done it all over again if I had had to. Nothing was worse than being unhappy and knowing there is more out there and not taking the risk. I remembered a line from a poem I once read, '*To risk nothing is to risk everything,*' and thought how true it was.

"I'm glad I left," I said at last, "I'm glad I didn't listen to all the people who told me not to try it, who told me to 'sit tight' and 'stick to what you know', who told me I had a good job and a nice house and I was mad to give it all up. Those who told me I would fail and come home miserable."

"Mmmmm," M agreed thoughtfully.

"There is something about the Belfast mentality that makes people very scared to venture into the unknown. I know what you mean by this 'sit tight' theory; you know, just stay put and count your blessings. It's almost as if the outside world is so threatening and terrifying that it is better to suffer badly paid jobs, all that tribal and religious shit and boring relationships than to change it. Perhaps it's lack of confidence."

"Yes and everything is a big deal," I added, "I heard the phrase 'I can't be bothered' so many times from people...'Oh I don't know how you could be bothered to uproot yourself and start again, I couldn't be bothered'...how can they be bothered to do *anything*?"

"It's so fatalistic. Accept your lot. Make your bed and lie in it. Must come from Catholicism," M said.

"Yep, don't try to change too much in this mortal life. After all, you get your rewards in the next one. Bullshit," I replied laughing.

"But look at us," she went on, "sitting on a sunny terrace in Delft, Holland, both with good jobs, places to live, friends, great futures, new men to discover," she winked in an exaggerated way at me and continued,

"And if it doesn't work out in the end; hell at least we tried, didn't we? We didn't 'sit tight' waiting for something to happen or waiting to die."

"Bravo!" I said and clapped.

M winked again and then I suddenly realised there was a gorgeous man standing right in front of me. I started and felt myself blushing.

"Excuse me *dames*, do you have a light for my cigarette?" He asked in English but with a slow Eastern European accent, emphasising heavily the *L* in light.

"Sure," I managed to say reasonably coolly and fumbled on the table for M's plastic lighter.

I handed it to him and he lit his cigarette. He had the most gorgeous heavy dark blue eyes I have ever seen. They were framed by thick sooty lashes, his nose rather large but his face chiselled and tanned and full of intelligence. His hair, short and stuck up at all angles as if he never combed it, was a kind of dark blondish, brown. He handed back the lighter and smiled.

"*Hvala*," he said and made a small bow, "and ciao, have a nice day."

M and I managed a nod and grinned like maniacs as he made his way across the square.

"I will have a nice day now," I said as I watched him stroll out of our lives.

"We should have chatted him up," M said, annoyed with herself for letting this opportunity pass.

"Too late now", I breathed feeling my heart rate return somewhat to normal, "Where do you think he is from?"

"*Hvala* means thank you in Serbian," M, The linguist declared.

"Serbia, conjures up fairy tale images of medieval castles, unicorns and long-haired maidens wearing pointed hats."

"And men like him climbing in to bed with you after a long hard day's work in a snowy field," finished M, still gazing into the distance.

We both laughed childishly.

"Now isn't being single fun? Contemplating all the possibilities," M said beaming and continued to gaze across the square until the figure slowly and lazily disappeared.

Chapter 9 – Beau

O Beau-tiful boy
Dark eyes
Beautiful mouth
You bit me when you kissed me
In your eagerness
And youth

I

The rest of the winter and even Christmas had passed in a blur of work and adapting to Holland. I had moved out of the VU accommodation and into a studio nearby in Amstelveen. It was quite cheap because it wasn't in the centre and it was convenient as I could bicycle to work in twenty minutes. The job at the VU was exhausting me so I had gotten application forms from most of the major international companies, Shell, OPCW, Europol and the Patent Office, to see if I could get an easier, better paid job. I reckoned I could get something better. I was tired of shift work, of having a sore back and being bossed around by nurses much younger than me. Even working in a bar had crossed my mind as being preferable to the hospital drudgery.

I was working hard decorating my studio with mismatched second hand furniture, coverings and pictures. I missed all my nice stuff in my old house. My Rosina Wachtmeister prints, my blue wooden cat, my tall umbrella plant with the white fairy lights and my green wicker coffee table, not to mention all the useful stuff like my sets of cooking pots, coffee machine, microwave, television and DVD player. All the stuff I'd forgotten about. It's funny how we cling to material stuff and think we can't live without them and a few months later we've forgotten they ever existed (if indeed pictures, pots and coffee machines do exist). But I longed to lie down in bed and watch an old film I loved, *The Sheltering Sky* or *Withnail and I*. Everything had to be bought again, from teaspoons to toilet brush, from bedding to blinds. But it was also wonderful fun. I could do exactly as I pleased. I bought some violet paint and covered the studio, ceiling and all. It looked fantastic, smaller but luxurious and warm, rich and royal like living inside a big Cadbury's milk chocolate bar. I bought a plant as large as I could carry and some pale pink fairy lights. Purple and pink. My childhood colours.

I had a small balcony which was crumbling and filthy and had a glorious view of a '70s style, socialist style housing block, but it caught the evening sun and I endeavoured to clean it, deck it out with hardy plants and put a little chair out in preparation for summer. The only thing missing was someone or someones to share it with. I wanted some visitors. Maybe I would invite some of my colleagues around for a drink. Saskia would come. But oh, what if no one else came? It wouldn't be a success like M's Halloween party. I sat down on the tired armchair which had come with the studio. I had been happily humming to myself, busy arranging this and that, hanging blinds, dusting forgotten corners but suddenly I felt flooded with doubts and fears. My confidence had taken a dive again. What was I really doing here? I had no real friends, a crummy studio. M was back in France. My family were in Ireland. I felt suddenly so small and alone and fragile that I thought I was going to cry.

I looked around my new purple paradise. It was a gorgeous mess of mismatched items of furniture and a riot of colour. It should please me very much but I suddenly felt empty and hurt and somehow ashamed. I was struck by such a pang of homesickness that it physically twisted my gut. All my childish feelings of failure, uselessness, shyness and ugliness came flooding back. They always did when I was at low ebb.

I also felt restless as if I was rushing headlong into something I didn't want to reach but I had no control to stop it. I felt everything was spiralling out of control, out of my hands. I felt as if I was strapped into a spaceship which was taking off with me and I didn't want to go. I didn't have any choice. It was my destiny and it was going to be very bad.

I stood up quickly and sharply reprimanded myself. I could feel my heart speeding up driven by some irrational fear-induced adrenaline surge. I felt a panic. Did I want to go home? If indeed it still was home. Had I had enough already? I knew I was being ridiculous.

I went to the window and looked outside. There was a soggy rectangle of patchy grass below which served as a park and dog toilet. A very skinny dog was urinating there, trembling with cold. I felt overwhelmed with pity and wanted to rush out and take it back here to the warmth. God, I was getting depressed. I looked beyond the park and the dog to the flats' curtained windows. What lay beyond? What suffering and cruelty and evil manifestations of the human soul presented themselves daily and nightly in those unseen, veiled rooms? How can people be happy when there is so much misery in the world? What a painful realization that we can never be happy whilst people and animals are still suffering around us. How our peace will be forever marred by the knowledge that there is pain and hurt and anguish going on behind closed doors and we cannot stop it.

How can I decorate my studio and enjoy its comfort and colour and light whilst somewhere at this very moment a skinny dog is trembling in the damp grass, shivering and hungry? Or a veal calf is standing on wobbly swollen arthritic legs in a dark crate. In abject, isolated misery.

How can I climb contented and secure into a warm bed whilst somewhere a little girl with big haunted eyes clings to her teddy bear in her own small bed while her overweight and crazed father rapes her? Is this happening somewhere right now as I stand and imagine it?

I sighed and turned away. This was just depressing me more. My thoughts were taking me on a dark trip. I was strapped into the spaceship again. But hey, the misery of the world was not going to stop by me getting depressed by it. Besides, it was a lovely spring evening. Chilly but still light. That lovely twilight, clear and cold, blue but pinkish. I shut the window. I sighed and went to the kitchen to prepare my dinner. No point in me being hungry too I thought. I put on some music, some light uplifting General Garcia. French, bubbly and chirpy. I took a leak from the shelf and a handful of dusty potatoes to begin my leak and potato bake and then smiled as I thought about M making me a variation of this dish during my first week with her in Reims.

She had rushed into the flat clutching a paper bag and excitedly proclaimed she'd been digging in Taru's mother's vegetable garden all day. As a reward she'd been presented with some fresh, organic, home grown produce. I got up to have a look and then burst out laughing as M magically unwrapped her wares which were two small, dusty carrots and a sad, shrivelled cabbage whereupon sat a huge, angry spider. She screamed and dropped the cabbage onto the floor and the spider scuttled off under the green counter. So much for all your hard work, I'd said still laughing partly now from nerves at having seen the spider. She glared at me and scooped up the cabbage.

"You'll see," she had said sniffing, "we'll have it for dinner and it will be delicious."

I rolled my eyes and began filling the basin with water to cleanse the cabbage of whatever other life forms dwelled within. The carrots, we agreed, were beyond redemption and were chopped up to be set on the window sill for the birds. Then M baked a cabbage and potato pie with parmesan cheese on top and it was the most delicious cabbage I have ever eaten.

After dinner, which was almost as nice as M's cabbage dish, I must have nodded off. I dreamed that a little blond boy of three or four was kissing me goodnight. He was wearing red pyjamas. He had fluffy hair and big, blue, china-doll eyes. He was my brother or my son. He kissed me on the lips and we both drew back suddenly laughing and said, "You taste like lemon," at exactly the same time. Then we began to laugh because we'd said the same thing. And I could taste his lemon in the dream, sweet and sour. Then I woke up suddenly, smiling but my phone was ringing chasing away the lightness of the dream. God, I thought, who even has my number?

It was Kristiana. I immediately had a vision of a whitewashed room and floating white curtains blowing in a soft breeze, before I wondered why on earth she would ring me.

Kristiana, I thought, shouldn't you be working on a new photography exhibition or at dinner with daddy's architect friends discussing contemporary interior design?

I lifted the receiver and spoke tentatively. "Hello."

"Oh Charlotte, M had an accident," she gushed in her smooth, European accent.

My knees turned to jelly and I dropped into the tired armchair. My scalp prickled and my stomach flipped. It felt as if some seconds had passed before I could say anything.

"Uh, huh, what happened?" I blurted finally," I mean, is she alright?"

"Oh yes, she's sitting here by me, us, she fell off her bicycle and banged her head, had a bit of concussion but refused to go to hospital and now we are sitting with her in case she vomits or has any of those neurological signs, you know," Kristiana rattled on consoling and gaining momentum now after frightening me to death with her opening sentence.

"Let me speak to her," I said sharply, angry now after my scare. I moved forward in the chair and began rearranging the things on the table beside me. Nail clippers, hand cream, hospital duty roster, tee-light, lighter.

"Of course, but she wanted me to dial for her," Kristiana answered, "she's fine really," she added as if trying to make up for scaring the hell out of me in the first instance.

M came on the phone moments later.

"I'm OK really," she immediately reassured me, "just a knock on the head. I didn't even want to tell you, you know and alarm you."

"What happened?" I asked beginning to relax. I picked up the lighter and began to flick it on and off.

"Oh, my bike chain broke," she continued, "it was very old and rusty...I was cycling by the canal and suddenly it snapped and I was flung backwards...landed on my back and banged my head."

"Oh my God, it sounds terrible, have you told daddy?"

"No, I don't want to worry him, besides I'm fine."

"But you should go to hospital for a check up. Get Kristiana to drive you. She has a car, doesn't she?" I added thinking that Miss Krissy should earn her friendship a bit.

"Nah, it's fine", M reiterated. "If I get a headache or vomiting I'll go."

"Or any visual disturbances," I added.

"It was bizarre," she continued, sounding a little bit excited now. "I was lying on my back by the canal and these people came over and started talking to me and I answered them but afterwards I couldn't remember if I'd been talking in English or French."

"Didn't they offer to take you to hospital?"

"No, I got up after a bit and said I felt OK, and I do... everyone is here keeping an eye on me, Kris, Guy, Taru, Angéline. If anything untoward happens they'll rush me to *l' hôpital, toute de suite*...got a big bump though."

"Well if you're sure you're OK, but take it easy and stop rushing around, OK?"

"I will, I will, I'm taking tomorrow off to relax and get my bike chain replaced,"

She sounded calmer now and there was a brief silence, then she began again.

"Hey, what are you doing for Easter?"

"Don't know."

And I did not know. Indeed I hadn't even thought of Easter. Christian festivals always seemed to slip my mind. The Pagan ones of *Samhain* and *Beltane* (May day) on the other hand, filled me with anticipation.

"I might come up," she piped all of a sudden and there was a long inhalation as she drew on a Gauloise at the other end.

"Sure," I said, trying not to sound delighted. "I painted my apartment purple," I added suddenly as if that would make up M's mind.

"Oh sounds gorgeous," she replied, exhaling now, "I'll call you when things are less confusing."

"Okay take care now, and remember, go straight to hospital if you get headaches or nausea, you know the thing...visual disturbance, dizziness and so on, oh and make sure someone stays with you," and I added 'not Kristiana' in my head.

M yeah, yeahed me, sang *au revoir* down the phone and we hung up.

I sat for a moment rearranging the things on the table again. Lighter, hand cream, tee light, hospital duty roster. It was April 2nd. Easter was on the 21st, my God I hadn't even thought of Easter. Time was hurtling by. Memories of new Easter clothes and chocolate eggs flitted through my head. Easter Sunday walks in the park. Feeding the ducks and realising the daffodils and crocuses were out and that the trees were green again instead of stark black. I smoked out of the window, blowing long tendrils of blue-grey out into the chilly twilight. The dog was gone from the waste ground below. I drew in and closed the window trapping raw spring air in my purple palace.

II

Standing at Amsterdam Centraal, shivering with a cardboard cup of espresso in both hands I waited for the Antwerp train to draw in to platform eight. M would be on it. It was the 14th April. She had recovered from her knock on the head and brought her Easter visit forward. It was great news. I had nothing else to do anyway and was glad of the company. M would come via four train changes. Reims to Paris, Paris to Lille, Lille to Antwerp, Antwerp to Amsterdam. She saved about 400 francs this way. I personally would have splashed out on the Thalys and sat rocking gently on red velour all the way through, dozing and waking, ordering some wine and a snack from the skinny, French steward who darted bird-like between the aisles. But M was M. Thrifty. Always saving for her future studies or travels. Maybe I should be saving for *my* future. But this *was* my future. Here I was in Amsterdam. God, it was cold for April.

The train drew in right on time and suddenly there she was, all red-faced and clambering out of the second class carriage, heavily encumbered with a massive blue rucksack, the old-fashioned, cheap, uncomfortable kind. God knows what she had in it. I dashed towards her waving and she saw me and waved back grinning broadly, her 'wicked pixie' grin. We clashed and hugged like two lovers at a station in a film. M smelled of leather, eucalyptus and mothballs. Her cheeks were burning hot.

"God you're warm," I said, "do you have fever?"

She smiled and shook her head, "of course not but sis, I'm glad to hear you are speaking English properly at last," she teased me.

I cocked my head, puzzled.

M's eyes were shining with mirth.

"Back in Belfast you would have asked, 'do you have a temperature', to which I would have replied, 'yes of course I have a temperature...everything has a temperature, 36.7 degrees, 0 degrees, 100 degrees,'" she began laughing.

I rolled my eyes and took her arm to steer her through the thronging crowd. One of the few things which irritated me so far about Holland was the amount of people in the cities. The station was literally teeming. Everyday was like a day out at the fair.

We went into a small brown-café for the obligatory coffee and exchange of up-to-date chat. It was so good to have her here again. I had been still feeling a bit lost. Tired of being alone and dealing with everything on my own. Then we checked her things in at my flat. The rucksack seemed to be mainly filled with dirty washing. I tutted as she dumped it unceremoniously onto the floor. She humphed as I told her I had no washing machine and she'd have to do it in the bath. I wondered why on earth she'd carted it all the way up here instead of doing it herself at home and then guessed that she had assumed that I had a washing machine. I shrugged inwardly and decided not to ask. My mental energy was better saved for the coming weekend. Sometimes M was difficult to fathom. It was all part of her charm.

Later we checked out the Café Lokaal. This had become one of my favourite dens in Amsterdam. It was all so unpretentious. It was in a cellar, dark, run-down, dusty and unclean, but the staff were always smiling, the beer was cheap, strong and cold and the music was great: grungy, rock, eighties pop, disco, they had it all. On some nights, local bands played there and even Spanish Flamenco dancers stomped their orthopaedic shoes on the bare boards once a week. I could go there and sit at the bar nursing a beer and feel completely relaxed. M and I went in too early and it was empty except for a few scruffy darts players sporting self-styled mullets and loafers minus socks. We ordered fine golden La Chouffe beer and babbled like sisters do, completely engrossed in meaningful conversation. At least to us it was meaningful. So engrossed we were, in fact, that at first I didn't even notice him, my Boy. He had walked in a few minutes ago and bought a very small beer which was mostly froth. No self-respecting Irish or English man would be seen drinking such a girly beer. But he didn't seem to care. He was tall. Very tall. Legs right up to his neck. He was smoking and strolled around first checking out the darts game, then the dance floor. Then he strolled into my view and I could not take my eyes off him.

M nudged me and grinned wickedly.

"I saw you looking," she whispered and giggled.

I gulped my beer nervously.

"He's fucking gorgeous," I rushed. I then had all the classic symptoms of the 'lightening strike'. Palpitations, sweaty palms, racing mammalian brain, probably dilated pupils. God I was actually shaking. I kept looking and he turned and looked back. And then he smiled: a gorgeous, slow, sexy smile and if I'd been standing up, my knees probably would have buckled.

"Go and talk to him," M urged under her breath and slurping her beer noisily, her eyes teasing my shyness.

"I couldn't," I said looking down at my beer, "I'll say something utterly ridiculous and he'll think I'm some sort of nut case."

"Besides," I went on, "he's way too young for me, looks about twenty, just a boy really."

M raised her left eyebrow quizzically.

"Well then go and chat up that young boy there before I do it for you," she said.

"No, he's far too good looking for me," I said teetering on the verge of doing just that then losing my nerve.

M tutted and tossed back her hair in a gesture of exasperation.

"You are beautiful, just as beautiful as him and he's looking at you right now and...," she continued, peering at him closely, "well he's not bad but he's not so good looking as that Serbian guy who asked us for a light in Delft."

"Oh him, yeah I remember him…" I trailed off because *he* was heading straight for me.

He had dark, very short hair which stuck up a bit at the front in a probably gel-contrived way and when he turned to me his eyes seems to burn me with their intensity. Great dark pools.

"Hi," he said, and offered his hand.

How polite, I thought, In Belfast he'd wait until he was so drunk he'd be almost ready to throw up, then launch himself across the dance floor, colliding with me and spilling my drink. His feeble ploy being to offer to buy me another and hence breaking the ice, my mammalian brain babbled.

"Beau," he said, "*wil je iets drinken?*"

I smiled. He smiled. 'Beau', I thought, 'of course you are'. I relaxed. M nudged me sharply.

"Yes thank you, I'll have another beer," I managed coolly.

"You're not Dutch," he said, switching to English delivered in a beautiful clipped, staccato accent.

"Well done," I said, smiling.

"OK, *grapjas*[6]," he said, smiling that lovely slow, sexy smile. Warm honey and cream.

"and your friend?" He glanced at M.

M shook her head.

"I have one already but thanks," M said more coolly than me.

I quickly drained my first La chouffe to justify having the one I'd just accepted from Beau.

We chatted for a very short time in reality, but it felt like much longer. My nerves left me after I while and I began to relax. Beau *was* just twenty, a chef and had just moved out from his mother's place. He had one brother and two sisters. He brought M into the conversation but didn't allow her to take over. This impressed me for I knew how difficult it was. He kept looking at me and smiling. He was polite and charming but I also felt he was very sweet and a little bit vulnerable underneath all that confidence. Sweet and maybe a little bit shy. Shyness more than compensated for

---

6. Dutch - Joker

by good manners and honed social skills. Irish men could really learn a thing from this twenty-year-old.

By the time he left, I was completely won over. I was already falling in love. Before he left he asked for my phone number. I recited it carefully leaving no room for error. I really wanted him to call me. He punched it expertly into this mobile phone along with my name which he managed to guess-spell correctly much to my astonishment, then hid it away again. Then he surprised me utterly. Just when I thought it couldn't get any better, Beau put his hands around my waist, grabbing gently the belt on my jeans, pulled me towards him and kissed me. His tongue played briefly in my mouth then it was over. It was just a short kiss. A young kiss which showed, for all his expert chatting-up skills, a distinct lack of experience. It was too fast and too strong and he bit my lip a little bit. But when it was over I was riding a roller coaster in my head and my emotions were spinning. Next time, I thought I'll teach you how to do it better.

Then he was gone and I started to wonder why he hadn't stayed longer and then my doubts and worries began their slow, merry dance in my head. What if he doesn't ring me? What if he *does* ring me?

M was grinning like a maniac beside me.

"Let's go somewhere else," she said getting up from the tall bar stool and rubbing her backside in a distinctly unfeminine way.

"Where to?" I asked, my eyes drifting hopefully towards the door. Maybe he would come back in again.

"Somewhere a bit more lively," M said and I followed her dutifully.

Much later we cycled home furiously for it was late and cold. M was babbling about someone in Sweden and about going up there for Easter. I was lost in the world of Beau.

I wondered was his saliva still on my lips. I could still taste him a little, a sweetness of aniseed and beer. All the way back to my purple paradise I was screaming inside, 'Oh my God! O my God! O my God!' and the smile across my face stretched my jaws until they began to ache.

But he didn't call me.

Sunday passed swiftly. M rushed around dragging me here and there. From the Van Gogh museum to the Anne Frank Huis. A Canal boat trip, ice cream in the Vondel park, a transvestite performing at the Dam Square. It was a welcome distraction for I could think of nothing else but Beau. Those dark eyes haunted my waking hours as well as my dreams.

The next few days were more relaxed and we chilled out at home.

The first few days are lovely when you fall in love. They pass in a whirl. Full of imagined telephone conversations, rehearsing for the big moment when they call you and ask you out on a date. Full of lying in bed or on the sofa looking out the window just dreaming of him, remembering every touch and look and word and smell. Breathing him in, in huge gulps and expiring slowly not wanting to let him go. Then the next few days you become restless.

He still hadn't called. It was Tuesday. M was dashing around the flat flapping dry, still damp clothes and tutting about my lack of a washing machine and dryer. But it all seemed to be happening far away. I could hear and see her but not really listening nor caring. Inside I was with Beau. I was playing out our meeting over and over again. His smile, his eyes, that kiss, the chemical and mental connection. But he hadn't called me. He had seemed so keen but now I was beginning to doubt it. All of it. He didn't like me after all. He was just playing the flirting game. Why the hell did he take my number if he wasn't going to call me? He didn't seem like the type to lack the courage. Maybe he would call at the weekend. Probably he didn't want to appear too eager. I tried to forget it but it was impossible. There was a seed of longing planted in my soul.

I was weary of thinking about him but I couldn't switch it off. My mind was running in circles like a wild horse in a small paddock.

M was sympathetic in an M kind of way. She shrugged.

"Holland is full of good looking guys," she tittered.

She was sitting on a damp towel trying to dry it with her body heat whilst rolling an elegant joint.

"I had noticed," I answered dryly.

"Especially the dark ones, the ones you like........ something about the eyes...plenty more fish in the sea," she continued not making me feel any better.

I sighed.

"Besides, maybe he'll call tonight or tomorrow. It's way too soon. He won't want to appear desperate."

Jesus, I thought, as if a guy like that could ever be desperate for female company. I'd be happy draped at his feet.

"He's young," M went on, now spreading the towel over her knees.

"He'll call on Friday night when he's had a few beers, a bit of 'Dutch courage'."

Maybe she was right. I had to relax about this.

When M was packed we left for the station. It was windy again. Everything was restless and moving, like my soul. It seemed like such a short visit and I felt a pang of regret and guilt for having been so preoccupied with Beau. But M was oblivious to my lack of attention. We hugged for affection and warmth.

"Don't forget to take your damp things out as soon as you get home," I ordered in a big sisterly, fake, stern tone.

She waved and called, "Yes mother, I'll see you soon."

"Yes soon," I replied, missing her already.

"I'll be back before you know it," she grinned and stepped into the second class, smoking carriage.

It was April 17th.

I never saw her again.

III

By Friday I was frantic. This was beyond cruel. Surely he would call before the weekend. Surely he would arrange something for Saturday night? I got home from the hospital ragged and exhausted and called my voice mail number even before I sat down. My heart began to speed up in anticipation of his call as it had already a hundred times that week. Maybe he called today and left a message, maybe this is the one. But instead I heard the familiar:

'Welkom bij KPN voicemail, u heeft geen nieuwe berichten,' said the automated Dutch woman on the recording. No messages. Oh if only she knew how that made me feel. Empty and despondent and tearful. I chided myself. I am a thirty year old woman. This guy is twenty. He told me so, completely unabashed and thinking it was quite a mature age to be. And in Holland I guess it is, when you are legally drinking in bars from the age of sixteen and not ever getting drunk.

I cannot allow this to take me over. I met a guy in a bar. He kissed me and took my number and now he doesn't call. No big deal. I can handle it. I have a life. Look on the bright side. Imagine if he did call and took me out for a few months and *then* didn't call. That would be much, much worse. So I have to content myself with letting it go, put it down to a nice experience and one which proves I am still attractive to younger men. But Oh my God, those dark eyes. I wished he'd been a little more ordinary. Then I wouldn't be so shaken up.

That weekend I resigned myself to the fact that Beau was not going to call me. I was going to be cool about the whole thing. Cool and mature and sorted. Then the following Friday I went to the café Lokaal to look for him. I berated myself the whole way as I rode my bicycle through the narrow streets crowded with Friday night revellers. They were full of couples and groups of friends and here I was, all alone. Going to sit alone in a bar like a sad, thirty-something hoping someone will talk to me. Then I was berating myself for berating myself. I am just going in for a beer. It's my favourite café and I can go there alone or otherwise as I damn well please. I don't give a shit who is there and who isn't and what they think. I thought of M and how she would behave. She'd shrug and toss her hair and say "It's his loss."

I took a deep breath and walked in, trying to look confident. I tried not to fiddle with my hair or touch my coat buttons as I tend to when I'm nervous. I went straight to the bar where there was a free stool, sat down and immediately regretted it. As I glanced around me, I saw the assembly of monsters who were perched there. One next to me grinned toothily and offered his hand. I turned away rudely but I wasn't going to speak to anyone tonight who I didn't want to. I only wanted my Beau but he wasn't there. He was somewhere in the big city and I may never see him again. This thought gave me a physical pang in my guts and I took a generous gulp of beer. Only these monsters were here to keep me company, these wolfish and leering predators. I felt small and miserable. My thin veneer of confident woman was peeling away rapidly like the old paper behind the bar. I stared at the string of tulip-shaped fairy lights there which were glowing red, orange and purple and tried not to catch the eye of the ogre next to me. I imagined Beau walking in, hugging me from behind and pressing his cool soft, aniseed-smelling cheek against mine.

I sighed and after a brief chat with the bar maid about the up and coming *koninginnenach* celebrations. The Dutch Queen Juliana's birthday. I finished my La Chouffe in one swoop and headed for the stairs. I wanted out of there. I wanted to breathe. The place had seemed so cosy when me and M sat there last week but now I wanted to run away from all those prying jackal eyes, 'go back to your wives and children', I thought.

I reached the top of the narrow cellar stairs and as I glanced at the doorway I nearly fell back down them again. I gasped audibly.

Beau was standing in the doorway talking on his mobile. There he was, all gangly limbs, dark eyes, black hair, beautiful mouth. I'd imagined him all week and he was even more gorgeous in the flesh than in my day dreams. He glanced at me, then quickly away. He didn't smile.

"Jesus, you are real," I managed to say. I heard my small voice in my head as if I was speaking from behind thick glass.

He turned to me and raised one eyebrow. He sighed and ended his call curtly.

"You gave me a false phone *nummer*," he said.

He put his mobile away and crossed his arms. Lithe, muscular arms but not too heavy.

"No... I gave you my number but you didn't call me," I said slowly not quite grasping what was going on but gradually realizing that maybe there could be some misunderstanding.

He took out the phone again. He pressed a few buttons and brought up my number. He began to read, "Charlotte, 066388545."

"This *nummer* is one digit too short," he said, irritated.

I clapped my hand over my mouth and suddenly began to giggle, understanding everything all at once.

"It's not a mobile number Beau, it's a land line, there's no 06 before it, just the city code 020 then the rest."

There was a brief pause during which both our minds caught up with the stupid mistake. How was it possible in this age of fast track, high tech communication that it could go so wrong?

"Shit," he said suddenly, lighting up, "I'm sorry. I'm stupid."

No, I thought, not stupid. Sexy and sweet and very young but not stupid. Just from another generation. Why would a twenty year old guy think of a land line? He probably had a mobile since he was ten. I was watching my first television programmes when I was ten. In black and white!

He started to laugh too. I looked into those exquisitely dark eyes and drank them in. I wanted to grab him and run off with him there and then. Take me with you Beau, take me anywhere but don't ever go out of my sight again. If I cannot look at you I think I'll die, I wanted to yell.

But it seemed I would have to let him out of my sight again because he was making a date with some friends who were going to Leiden that evening. I didn't have the nerve to ask if I could come. But then in a rush of confidence I said, "Tell you what, you give me *your nummer* and we'll start again."

I fumbled around in my bag for a pen and scrap of paper and I watched in disbelief, heart pounding as he wrote his number and email address for me. We kissed on the cheek three times, his hand briefly touched my shoulder and then he was gone.

"Fuck!" I said out loud, staring at the small piece of crumpled card in my hand.

Beau looked back smiling then he disappeared.

The next day I got up late feeling washed out and un-rested but full of adrenalin thinking about the previous nights events. I couldn't wait to tell M. I had *his* number. I could pick up the phone any time I wanted to and hear that low, 'honey and cream' voice. No more waiting around by the telephone. No more empty voice mailbox. No more rushing home from work to disappointment and an empty flat.

I had the power. In my hands lay the key to my happiness in a new country. My first date with Beau. I sighed with delight and pulled the thin curtains open to let in a trail of exhausted, spring sunshine.

I luxuriated in the bath thinking about him and planning where to go what to wear what to say. I lit candles and breathed in warm wax and faint lavender. I wondered who he was, about his family, how many girlfriends he'd had, what he loved, what he hated, what were his passions. Now I loved Holland. At that moment, that morning in April, in Amsterdam I was utterly joyous. I felt like the worst of the settling in was over. I was putting down roots. I was never going back home. I *was* home.

I dozed off in the bath and dreamed of him. It was my first dream in the Dutch language. We were on my sofa. I was sitting up. He was lying with his head on my lap. I was playing with his soft near-black hair. We were laughing. The dream was full of warmth, love and peace. Then I asked him, "*Hoe goed zie je kleuren?*"

He laughed.

"*Veel mannen zien kleuren niet goed, veel mannen zijn kleurblind*," I went on as if to explain my strange question. It was strange, after all to ask someone how well they could see colours then explaining that many men are colour blind, but in the dream it was perfectly logical.

Beau didn't answer and as I continued to play with his hair it began to change colour from black to purple, a kind of grape-black. And then suddenly it was not his head on my lap but a soft black cat; a grape-coloured cat. I continued stroking it but it leapt up and ran away.

I woke up very cold and got hastily out of the bath.

I decided to call him on Thursday evening. I felt that I would not appear too desperate if I left it till later in the week and yet there would still be enough time to plan a Friday or a Saturday date, however I was itching to ring him. I did everything to distract myself from thinking about him. I rang Saskia and we met at the Waterlooplein Market, had a boozy lunch and ate *vlaamse frites* at the Dam Square watching the American tourists go by loudly complaining about the service they'd just had at some restaurant. We wandered around the Red Light District chatting and glancing shyly in the windows where beautiful young girls sat perched on stools like bored birds of paradise. And some not so beautiful, older, fatter ones sat with their knitting, looking decidedly unenthused. Saskia and I giggled at this. We were becoming really good friends and I regretted her not having met M. I wanted to show off my sister and I wanted her to see I could have friends too and not pretentious ones like sailing girl, Kristiana. I told Saskia about Beau and she sighed in longing. She was rather plump and homely looking, though not unattractive. She had dark glittering eyes and a lovely smile but confessed she'd never had much luck with men. I told her she should try boys.

I worked on Sunday afternoon even though it was my weekend off but they needed extra hands and it was a good way of making the time go by more quickly. Jeroen, the head nurse said I looked different and I told him I had met someone. I blushed as I told him about Beau and he teased me and went away whistling the tune to *love lifts us up*, announcing loudly and much to my embarrassment that I was in love.

I wheeled old ladies into the shower, hoisted them out of their sweaty night things and onto the toilet. I made beds. I wheeled beds around. I disinfected night stands. I gave out juice and tea and medications. I wrote reports and took phone calls and forgot to put my verbs in at the end in Dutch sentences. I sat with relatives and watered flowers, patted children and hummed merrily to myself all the while. I looked at the old patients in pity and wondered what sort of lives they'd had. I hoped they had taken risks and jumped at chances. I hoped they had lived every minute of every day as if it was their last. I hoped they had loved and lusted and suffered from it. But alas as I talked to them and learned all too often of young marriage to unsuitable men and many years of rearing ungrateful children. They'd had no time to travel, no money to study for a career, no independence, no rich recklessness. I hoped that when I was old and being wheeled around a nursing home or hospital that I had stored up enough life to have something to smile about when smiling was all I *could* do.

Saskia and I went to four o'clock coffee break together and I was so tired I felt sick. I hadn't been sleeping again and felt like a child the night before Christmas. What was Beau going to think when he sees me looking like an old woman? I thought as I caught sight of myself in the glass fridge door. My hair was dry and frizzy and needed cutting, my skin was papery and dry. I had dark circles under my eyes. My mouth seemed to be migrating downwards giving up its weary battle against gravity. My God he'll run away from me. I looked every day my full thirty years (and more). In fact I was only two weeks off my thirty-first birthday.

M would be in Sweden on my birthday. I had been a bit peeved at first but she really wanted to go there and besides it was my thirty first not my twenty first. No big deal. Too many birthdays already. Maybe Beau would take me out or, in these days of equality, I could take him out. Or we could go Dutch, I mused.

It wasn't the fact that M was possibly going to Sweden that bothered me, but the fact that she was going with and to stay with some pretty dreadful people. Kristiana-types. Actually the sailing girl herself was probably going. But Kristiana never decided to do anything until the last moment. It was, according to her, uncool to arrange things too far in advance. She would decide a few days before and daddy could pick up the bill of the flight booked hours before departure. She didn't seem to realise that apart from the money it was damned inconsiderate to keep on dithering about when and where. M said I was getting old when I explained this. She told me to relax and chill and to stop being neurotic. That shut me up. If there is one thing I am scared of being (apart from ordinary) it is neurotic.

Neurotic conjures up images of middle aged women in curlers following their husbands around with damp clothes in case of accidental spillage. Flowery-cardiganed, big-buttocked women scrubbing their front steps and doors as if their lives depended on it and as if their whole moral being would be judged on the shininess of their door knockers. Women who get food processors and steam irons for Christmas (and are thankful for them). Not me, I thought. Not me who has a date with a gorgeous Dutch boy ten years my junior. I can go home to my own place, do exactly as I please, having to answer to no-one. It felt good. It felt exactly like me. I felt the now familiar butterflies in my stomach whenever I thought of Beau. It was exciting but I wished I could settle and get a good night's rest. I was waking up two or three times in the night and couldn't get back to sleep for ages. This was getting ridiculous and I wished I had some drug I could knock myself out with and sleep for ten hours.

That Sunday night I sat up until I was battling to keep my eyelids even half open. I drank a glass of rather rough brandy and smoked a joint. If I don't sleep tonight I think I'll die tomorrow, I thought as I climbed into my little *twijfelaar* (doubter; not a single, not a double) bed and thought about waking up at half past six the next morning with a whole week of work ahead of me.

I remembered nothing until the alarm clock blasted me out of my sleep-cocoon. I woke suddenly but felt blissfully refreshed and cleansed. I lay in the dark for a few moments thinking immediately of Beau and his dark eyes and long black lashes. I felt healed from all the trauma of moving and breaking relationships; new people; new job and all the other little things that go with living in another country like opening a bank account or getting a telephone connected. Hell even going to the supermarket could leave me bereft of energy and confidence at times. Maybe I was finally at peace just being here by myself. But I knew it was meeting Beau that had made me feel like this and I also knew that he could already hurt me by not phoning or not showing up on a date. But it was too late for all that. I was ready to fly again. In fact I had already jumped off the cliff and if I was going to be hurt on the way down or at the bottom then I was going to be hurt. But I was not missing the free-fall. Not for anything.

IV

It was April 28th. It was almost three weeks since I met him in the café. It was getting warmer. I was noticing all the spring signs, the crocuses, the narcissus and the tulips. Holland was full of flowers in spring. It was the most gorgeous place to be in the world when the tulips were everywhere in full bloom and glorious colours from purple-black to orange, yellow and red. And I was falling in love so all my senses were heightened. The colours smells and textures of everything were luxurious.

I had had a date with Beau. I had phoned him on the Thursday like I planned. He had sounded enthusiastic about meeting up and a little bit nervous. He laughed a lot and talked much too fast in Dutch a lot of which I didn't understand. But we arranged to meet on the Saturday. We went to The Dizzy Duck, a cosy coffee shop, and chatted in a mixture of English and Dutch. When he got tired speaking English, Beau reverted to Dutch sometimes in mid-sentence. It was always a little too fast for me but I was getting used to his voice and rhythms of speech. When I got tired speaking Dutch I reverted to English taking pains to modify my accent and speak clearly for him. We talked over each other at times and at other times there was a long silence when we just looked at each other. He kissed me again suddenly as we talked and I felt his heart beating really fast in his chest, even faster than mine and when he lifted his glass to take a sip of beer, his hand was shaking visibly. Beau, for all his bravado that night we met, was actually a little bit shy. He confessed he had smoked some 'weed' that night and would not normally have been so spontaneous. I was glad he had behaved spontaneously with me that night.

I was so attracted to him that by the end of the evening when he asked me back to his room, I just couldn't say no. I felt 'easy' going back to a guy's place on the first date. But this felt special. And we both knew it wasn't going to be just for a coffee and a goodnight kiss.

I stayed the night in his bed, his arms wrapped around me, lost in each others skin and smells and rhythms. We made love and when we were tired, we just lay there with eyes shut, sometimes open. I couldn't stop looking at him. His dark lashes lay against his face like miniature lopsided smiling crescent moons. I lay sometimes looking at him and sometimes gazing at the string of red fairy lights he had strung across his empty fireplace. I turned away from him with his arms wrapped around my chest and his cheek against my shoulder.

I was vaguely aware that I had had some sort of existence up until this point and vaguely aware that I would again in the morning but that blissful night there was no past or future for me. There was only the present. The listening to the sound of heavy rainfall on his window whilst watching the shadows on the yellowing wallpaper. The listening to him breathing and knowing he wasn't asleep. And nor was I that night. I never wanted it to end. All the nightmares of the past months were washed away by that one night in the arms of my beautiful boy.

It was the calm before the storm.

I got back to my purple studio on Sunday evening. I was walking on air and grinning like an idiot. I hummed merrily as I made a cup of tea. I slumped on my chair and lifted the phone to check my voice mail. I made a mental note to get a mobile. Then I could send Beau text messages and keep in touch all day. I was missing him already and the depth of my feelings was beginning to scare me a little.

There was one message from M.

"*Hola, ma petite soeur*, I'm off to Sweden tomorrow night. I'm staying outside Stockholm...mmm... I guess you've been seeing some dark-eyed boy this weekend," she giggled, "ooh la la...anyway this means I won't see you on your birthday but Kristov really wanted me to come." There was a pause and I guessed she was inhaling a cigarette. "His friend's band is playing on Tuesday night and...oh, I have to dash, the doorbell is ringing...see you soon and happy birthday, oh I'm ringing at six on Saturday evening." Then she hung up.

I felt immediately a pang of disappointment. I wanted to see my sister on my birthday. I wanted her to come out with Beau and me. I wanted her to really meet him. Now she would be up in Sweden with those pretentious pseudo-rock stars and probably the dreadful Kristiana though she hadn't mentioned her. I sighed and closed my eyes, the rim of the cup on my lip, the steam soothing my tired eyes. I inhaled deeply and realised that I was being selfish. Why would she want to hang around with a couple when she could be with a group of friends in a cool city? I listened to M's message one more time then erased it and then for some reason, I wished I hadn't.

Chapter 10 – *Beltane*[7]

I

M was in Stockholm. She was standing at the station smoking a rolled up cigarette and looking at her watch. She had travelled alone. Kristiana hadn't turned up after all. M had shrugged. She didn't like Kristiana that much anyway but it was someone to hang around with. M's breath left her body in huge puffs of white smoke, partly frozen exhalation and partly rough tobacco smoke. She didn't wear gloves and her hands were reddened by the cold. She wore only a green, thin, second hand leather jacket and jeans. All around her Swedes bustled about in woolly hats, fur trimmed coats and knee high boots. This was Sweden in late April and it was white cold.

She looked at her watch and then suddenly picked out a face in the crowd. Someone she knew. It was Kristov. He waved frantically at her and started to run towards her.

"Big hug darling, *mwah*," he said, wrapping his skinny arms around her and making the sound of an exaggerated kiss. M hugged Kristov back and grinned form ear to ear.

"How was the flight *dahling*?" Kristov gushed, throwing a skinny arm around her shoulder and steering her towards the exit.

---

7. *Beltane* - Irish Gaelic - Pagan Spring/May day festival (pronounce Bel-tan)

"Fine, bit of turbulence, two gins fixed that," M smiled.

"I hate flying too", Kristov said spitting the word hate and grimacing as if mentioning the activity was somehow almost as unbearable as doing it.

They reached the exit of the train station and stood outside a little while whilst Kristov took a cigarette from his suede jacket and lit it, looking around deciding which was the best way to Voljoer, the village where he lived.

"Shall we take the tram, it's lovely and scenic route, only takes half an hour. My mother has made tomato soup for you and there's salmon and breads and yummy things, she's really looking forward to meeting you," Kristov gabbled.

M shrugged.

"It's your city, let's take the tram then. Your mother shouldn't go to any trouble on my account," she continued, but was secretly pleased that Kristov should be so well prepared for her visit.

"She's my mother," he grinned, "it's *expectable.*"

M clamped her hand over her mouth, stifling a giggle.

"You mean, expected," she laughed, eyes twinkling with mirth and mischief and the icy air.

Kristov coloured slightly and smiled.

"Oh, I can see I'm in for a week of having my English corrected M, let's see how your Swedish compares."

"Your English is usually impeccable, Kristov," M said, "and by the way, been *on* any good parties lately?" she added unable to resist teasing him about a previous funny mistake he had made.

He shook his head and drew heavily on his cigarette.

"Yes my dear I have been *on* a few outrageous events of late," he laughed good- naturedly.

Kristov steered M onto the green and white Stockholm tram and they travelled to Voljoer.

II

Plop, plop, plop went the rain. It was falling heavily and dripping off my window ledge and onto the wooden balcony roof of the downstairs flat making fat, plopping sounds. It was comforting in a way but I was miserable now that I was awake. Beau hadn't phoned me. It was Wednesday and I had last seen him on Sunday morning after spending the night. I awoke from some unpleasant dream to a more unpleasant reality and my stomach lurched as I remembered him. First sweetly, his lovely solemn dark eyes and his sensual lips and pale skin contrasting beautifully with his thick dark hair, almost black, but not. Then I hitched my breath in stark realisation that he hadn't phoned me and he had promised. He had promised to see me on my birthday and he hadn't even bothered to call me. Now it was 3rd May, one day after my birthday.

I sighed and pulled the covers up around my head wanting to cry again. My eyes were already sore and puffy from the previous night. I had cried myself to sleep like a child, berating myself for getting so miserable over someone I hardly knew and for being a thirty (now thirty-one even) year old woman in love with a twenty year old child who only wanted sex and nothing else. How could I be so stupid? So naive? Why would he want a relationship with me? How could I imagine he wasn't only after the physical stuff? All the chatting up, the kisses, the looking into my eyes, stroking my hair, telling me I was beautiful. All that energy and deceit for one night of physical gratification. I suppose he thinks it was worth it. It was only making love after all. Except I didn't get any love. Only that which I had imagined.

A fresh wave of sympathy washed over me and I remembered I now had four days off work. Much as I hated it, at least it was a distraction from Beau whose image haunted me day and night. Now I had four days to wallow around my flat in my own misery. M was in Sweden. I had no friends except maybe Saskia, here. No one I could really call up on short notice. No one I knew well enough to comfortably open my heart to and share my misery with.

How cold now were the waters of my freedom. How I had languished on the ship of security feeling stifled and bored and shackled, tentatively looking over the edge but scared to jump. How dull had seemed my old comfortable relationships. The family visits, the cosy, secure and the predictable. My prison wardens. How I had wanted to jump and so many times had floundered on the deck, a prisoner of my own lack of courage, looking over the rails and then running back down into the bowels of the ship where it was warm and safe even though I couldn't breath there and knowing that within a few days, I would want to jump again.

And then one day I *had* jumped. And now this was how the waters could be. Freezing cold. Empty. I could drown in them.

I dragged myself into an upright sitting position, sheets still wrapped around me. I had to go on I guess. Have a shower, eat, tidy-up, everything mechanical. No more smiling to myself like an idiot all day, dancing and singing around the flat or in work. Back to the daily grind. Oh, but how I wished I'd never met him. I was stirred up. How cruel of him. How I hated him. And how I loved him.

I managed to get dressed and make some sort of a breakfast. I chewed soft toast like a robot whilst a big salty tear rolled down my nose and landed on the bread. I wasn't hungry and my stomach was tensed into a tight knot. The mushy bread seemed to grow in my mouth and I had to force it down. I slurped my tea whilst sobbing in great gusts. I almost choked. I didn't care.

Then I started making excuses for him. May be he lost my number? Maybe something has happened. Maybe he had an accident. Oh my God or someone died? Maybe I was being cruel, horrible, selfish and insecure. Maybe he would call me today or tomorrow? But I knew in my heart of hearts that Beau had gotten what he wanted and bolted. I was a fool. And it hurt.

I sat a long time staring out the window at the rain. I lacked the energy to do anything else. It was grey, dull day. The sky seemed somehow low and oppressive like my mood. I kept trying to think about doing something. I should go to the internet café and look up the films, treat myself to a cosy afternoon at the cinema. I could go to the library and get some trashy fiction, lose myself in it. But as every thought began, it turned to him. His eyes. His smile. His touch. His voice. How cute he had looked on Sunday morning in his black jeans and red fleece with the hood. How he had hugged me from behind as I made tea in his little kitsch kitchen. How I had thought, how gorgeous is this guy standing by the bar in the Dizzy Duck café, then gulped at the realisation that he was with *me*, waiting for me to bring our beers from the bar. He had smiled and we clinked glasses and he had asked me again how to say cheers in Irish.

"*Sláinte,*" I said.

"*Slesha,*" he said, pronouncing it all wrong. Cute.

I blinked and my eyes were filling with warm tears again. Lost in another Beau day dream. I was going crazy. I only went out with him once. What was wrong with me? I must be mentally unhinged. But maybe I should ring him? I had his number. But no, I thought, if he really wants me he has to call, otherwise I'll never know. And I could not shake off the feeling that it was over before it had really begun.

Suddenly the phone rang and my heart sped up into overdrive. Shit maybe it's him. I didn't want to answer it in case it wasn't. I somehow couldn't bear the disappointment but unable to resist, I picked up the receiver.

"Hallo, Charlotte speaking," I said, my voice cracking on the second syllable of my name.

There was silence on the line. Outside a small dog yapped in the rain. I repeated, stronger this time.

"Hallo, Charlotte speaking, who's there?" I asked.

There was an audible click on the end as the caller hung up. Shit! Was it him? Was he scared, nervous, shy? Was it a wrong number? Why would Beau call me then hang up? Was he cut off? I wished I could climb inside his head for five minutes and find out the answers to all my questions.

I shuffled into the bathroom and slapped on some make up but I didn't care how I looked. I looked how I felt. Exhausted and rejected. My eyelids were purple from crying. My head thumped. I looked like a kicked dog. I remembered Kristiana that day, long ago it seemed, in the corner Bistro in Montmartre on her spiel about treating waiters with contempt. "If one acts like a dog one is apt to be kicked," she had said basking in her own self satisfaction. Yes I had been kicked. A big kick in the teeth. I had briefly stood shining on my pedestal then it had been kicked out from under me. Hard.

Suddenly I had to know. I didn't care any more. I would call him and get the truth. I couldn't stand this hanging on one moment longer.

I picked up the telephone my hand shaking and punched in his mobile number. I cleared my throat and tried to summon up some confidence. After all I was just a confident, independent, thirty- one year old casually calling a boy. I was an adult for Christ's sake. What did I have to lose? Maybe I had it all wrong after all.

It rang once, twice, three times. I was ready to hang up when he answered.

"*Hallo met Beau,*" came the deep slightly hoarse voice on the other end.

Planets away.

"Hey *schat*, it's me, Charlotte," I managed trying to sound casual and then hating myself for calling him sweetie.

Silence. I heard the dog yap again.

"Oh hi, how are you?" He said switching to English. I immediately knew by the tone of his voice that it was over. It was cold and a little impatient.

Music was playing in the background. The non specific thud of processed disco from a café or pub. Voices babbled. Laughter rose and fell.

I guessed he was at work. He worked in a café kitchen.

"Fine," I lied, my voice audibly shaking, "I didn't hear from you, I wondered how you are doing."

"Good," he said.

Silence again. Beau coughed. Then,

"Actually...I'm very busy, maybe I can call you back."

My stomach lurched and I hitched in my breath. I lost my cool.

"Great," I said, "but when do I see you again?"

Silence again. The line crackled. I held my breath.

"Dunno," he said finally.

"Dumped," I thought, "you are so dumped my girl, *so* dumped."

"Oh maybe we should just forget it then," I managed beginning to get angry. Emotion rising in my voice and knowing I should just said OK and hang up but going on, making it worse.

Silence again. I knew what the answer was going to be but it was still a shock when I heard it.

"Yeah I think it's better," he said with a sigh.

A woman's laughter in the background.

This, from the guy who held me tight all night last Saturday and asked me please not to leave. This from the guy who stroked the small of my back and asked if he could see me again. This from the guy who kissed my eyelids in his kitchen.

Better than what? I thought. Better not have a girlfriend ten years older than you hanging round your neck. Better you had a good time, chalk it up on your bedpost and move on to securing the next one.

I hung up. Fresh tears streamed down my face. Tears of anger and frustration and hurt. Tears of anger at myself for getting carried away about a guy his age and for letting him hurt me.

Tears falling around me in the waters of my freedom. I could drown in them.

III

It was now dark. I had gone out and done some shopping, essentials like bread and milk. I didn't want to eat but supposed it was necessary. I was more abjectly miserable than I had ever been in my whole life. How I wished M was here. Anyone.

I lay on the lumpy sofa and curled up into a ball. I somehow drifted into a semi-dream state recalling a time in my childhood when I had once almost drowned in the sea.

I relived the event vividly bit by bit. I was twelve or thirteen. We were on holiday in Donegal. We were on the beach and it was warm enough to swim, though the waters of the Atlantic are always cold.

Green. The sea was green, sky blue and turquoise blue. Farther out it lay glittering like a dark, enchanted sapphire. I waded out into the surf. The surf was high and foamy and sparkling white. I was well within my depth for I was scared to actually swim in the sea. I had also been sternly warned by my mother not to go too far. I didn't. I was jumping the waves. They hit me from behind one after the other. It was windy, very windy and the wind whipped the foam from the surf and tossed it onto the white sand. Then a huge wave hit me and knocked me off my feet. I screamed at first with delight, then with terror. I went under and then I tried to get up. I had lost my feet and couldn't feel the bottom. I was in sheer mammalian panic. I tried to get up again, tried to find the sea floor. I couldn't. I thought of my parents, of M, of my body being found weeks later floating and bloated on some far shore. I started to lose my breath. I had to breathe. I had to get up but the water was all around me, above and below. I could feel the current pulling me farther under. I thrashed my arms and suddenly I was up. I gasped. Suddenly I could get my feet on the bottom. A new wave had brought me back into my depth. The beach had shelved and the combination of that and the rip tide had pulled me under and out away from the beach. I saw my father run towards me. His strong arms grabbed me and carried me to the shore. I was howling from terror and relief. He laid me on the sand and I vomited copious amounts of salty water. I lay there shaking and crying for quite a while. My father held me in his arms. M sat beside me, looking curiously at me, one hand on her green plastic beach spade and the other on my head.

IV

"Have you been up all night?" Kristov asked, surprised as he wandered into the polished pine kitchen to make coffee.

M was seated in the old beige armchair. Eyes open. Wide-awake. She did not smile nor acknowledge him.

It was 7 a.m. the day after she arrived.

The kitchen clock ticked loudly. Light snow tapped on the window.

She looked pale and strange and tired.

Then she turned to him and grinned an intense grin. It was however, too false, too strained. She tilted her head at him, almost leering, "Tick tock, tick tock", she said, then laughed.

Kristov smiled uneasily. M was acting a little bit strangely since she had arrived in Sweden, but they had had quite a lot of champagne the night before. Probably she was still a little bit drunk.

He sat down on the beige sofa opposite her, knees up against his chest hugging them. His shoulder length blond hair was unkempt and sticking out at the back. M thought he looked cute, innocent and freshly washed.

"You liked my friends?" he asked, deciding to ignore the 'tick tock'.

M nodded enthusiastically and seemed to be returning to the here and now. She looked out the window at the snow which was falling heavily and steadily now. There was already a thin layer covering the grass like frosting on a cake.

"Yeah they're really cool, especially Anouk, she's a sweetheart."

Kristov switched the radio on. Swedish pop music played. The coffee was ready. He got up pulling his long sweatshirt down over his thighs and shivering slightly. Barefoot, he padded across the kitchen. Thin blond hairs stood up on his legs.

"Isn't it funny how everything is round?" M said suddenly cocking her head again to one side.

"Huh?" he mumbled.

"I mean, the earth, all the planets, the egg, life, the whole cycle, its round," M explained.

Kristov shrugged.

"I never really thought of it."

"Ha, of course you did, you just didn't realise it. Think about it," M said sitting upright now in the chair and frantically twisting a strand of hair. "the cycle of life, it's spherical, the planets, my eggs in my ovaries waiting to be changed into new life, it all just goes around and around, spinning planets, birth and death, chicken and egg."

"Yeah I guess, spinning, turning, recycling," he repeated pouring two cups of coffee. "It kind of scares me though, thinking of all that blackness out there. That we are sitting here on a spinning rock, suspended in space in an infinite universe." Kristov shuddered and carried the coffee to M who was bolt upright now and slightly flushed. Her eyes were wet with excitement. Her face shone.

"Doesn't scare me," she said cupping her hands around the hot coffee, "I find it infinitely fascinating."

Kristov nodded and sipped his coffee tentatively.

"Infinity is infinitely fascinating. They say there are as many universes as there are bubbles in a shaken bottle of beer."

He looked distractedly out at the snow.

"It makes me insecure," he added laughing. "I feel I might fall off and and…and…...there's nothing holding us up. Gravity keeps us on board and spinning creates gravity but what if the spinning stops?"

M frowned. "Then it's the end of the world. Then we fall off," she said flatly.

Kristov laughed but it was a nervous laugh. He didn't like the way she looked. Spaced out. Distant. Scared almost and her mood was swinging from a kind of manic intensity to a flat despair minute to minute.

He sipped his coffee.

"Are you OK, M?" He asked casually but looking directly at her blue-grey eyes. They looked heavy and sad.

She shrugged.

"I feel a bit weird Kristov," she said at last looking like some semblance of her usual self.

"I can't find the lines any more."

"How do you mean?"

M shrugged again.

"You know, the lines, the guides, the rules, the physics...I've sort of lost them. What's real and what's not."

Kristov stood up and walked over to her chair. He kneeled down beside her and put his blond head in her lap one arm around her back and one on her knees.

M stroked his soft, sticking-out hair and sighed.

"I think I know what you mean," he said.

"Reality," M said still stroking his hair.

"I can't find the lines between fantasy and reality...it's getting mixed up, merging somehow."

Kristov lifted his head and fixed his slightly oriental blue eyes on her.

"You're scaring me," he said.

"I'm scaring myself," she answered.

"Maybe you're just tired, burned out and need to rest.... maybe you're having a kind of *crise de nerfs,*" he added, trying to giggle a little at the French phrase that always conjured up images of powdered ladies in tightly laced-up corsets being fanned back to life and given smelling salts after hearing the news that there was only one fish course that evening at dinner.

The phrase trivialised the condition.

Kristov sat himself up and ran his fingers through his hair.

"We can just chill out here today if you like. I'll bake some biscuits or something, we'll have hot chocolate...maybe build a *lumiukko* outside if it keeps snowing like this," he said

What's a *lumiukko*? M asked.

"A snowman silly," he said, "a Swedish snowman....a magic one. Well, actually it's Finnish for snowman not Swedish but enough of the technicalities."

So as it continued to snow heavily, after coffee which was black and sweet and strong, M and Kristov went outside into the garden and crispy white snow. They both donned thick ski-jackets (borrowed from his mother) and hats, scarves and gloves. The snow was falling steadily and M stuck out her tongue to catch it. It melted at once into cold, slightly metallic-tasting water. The trodden impacted snow squeaked underfoot as they rolled it into two large balls and began to build the lumiukko. M looked more like her usual self as they laughed and chatted unselfconsciously like two old friends. Her strange outburst of abstract thoughts were seemingly forgotten. Her eyes shone and two dark spots of red appeared high on her cheekbones from cold and exertion.

M was packing the snow into a shape resembling a somewhat disfigured snowman and glancing every now and then up at Kristov trying to work out whether or not he was good looking. He had a strange face, she thought. Not conventionally handsome but somehow compelling. The nose was too large, the mouth too large, red and mobile. He was so blond as to be almost featureless. Pale, palest eyebrows and lashes giving his face no frame, no structure. His best feature, his shoulder length blond hair was now hidden under a woolly hat and what could be still seen was dark and lank in the damp air. But his eyes were beautiful. Sky blue and intense and slightly tilted up as if there had been some distant Asian ancestry. A Chinese or Indonesian great grandparent who left their subtle mark. Their genetic immortality. And he was short. Not much taller than M who stood at the grand height of 167 centimetres. He was thin and lithe and M guessed there was not an ounce of fat on that hard, wiry body.

Suddenly she wanted to kiss him. Wanted to feel those generous lips on her mouth, squeeze herself against that firm boy's body and look into those intelligent blue eyes.

"What's you lookin' at?" Kristov said smiling noticing the attention, "keep going, he's nearly done."

Kristov's teeth on the bottom were small and too many. Some of them crossed over each other like crooked tombstones in an overcrowded cemetery.

"I was just thinking you are actually quite cute," she said suddenly and without thinking.

"Actually?" he said grinning widely and began gathering armfuls of snow and making snowballs. He ran at her with one and threw it wildly and inaccurately missing by a mile. M ran clumsily away in the thick snow, her arms over her head and ducked exaggeratedly and unnecessarily.

They stopped and stood looking at each other, gasping for breath. Kristov dropped his ammunition and dusted off the powder snow from his gloves and jacket now looking slightly embarrassed. Then in an effort to regain his dignity, put his hands on his hips and cocked his head to one side.

"Gee thanks kid, I'm not you know, but thanks," he said.

M cocked her head the other way and screwed up her face.

"Nah, you're right" she said, "you're not...I was high on snow, forget it."

Kristov threw his head back and laughed.

"Lumiukko's cute though," he said nodding to the misshapen snowman, "maybe we should build him a mate."

"Better make him a face first...go get a carrot or something," M suggested suddenly conjuring up childhood images of backyard snowmen with orange carrot noses and black coal chip eyes.

Kristov looked up at the low grey sky which was full of the promise of more snow. It was falling now thicker and faster and it was becoming difficult to see.

"Mmm," he said thoughtfully

"I have a better idea...like hot chocolate with whipped cream, or I know, let's make rice porridge."

M raised her left eyebrow quizzically.

"Lumiukko. Rice porridge. This is turning into a real cultural experience. Two things I've never heard of in one afternoon. OK, sounds like a good idea in this weather and maybe while you're at it you can tell me some old Swedish folk tale or sing a song about killing whales on the sea ice."

Kristov tutted.

"I think you'll find that you are thinking of Norwegians my dear."

They went inside, shaking snow everywhere and leaving huge wet footprints on the wooden floor in the hallway.

Kristov put the rice porridge on the stove to simmer.

"This is traditionally *wot* one eats on Christmas morning in Sweden. It needs a lot of attention to stop it burning since the rice is boiled entirely with the milk," he began in an exaggerated English accent.

"It's just rice pudding then," M said curtly, peering into the pan.

Kristov ignored her and carried on.

"One gets up very early usually, just as Santa Claus is leaving, to soak the rice in milk and then begins gently to heat it over a low flame being *ex-tweemly* careful not to let the rice stick or burn. One must continually stir the mixture for at least twenty minutes until the rice is soft but one musn't let it burn or it's ruined."

M sat down on the couch to prepare a cigarette. She closed her eyes. She felt very happy but her head was recently whirling with strange thoughts. She tried to push them away but they persisted, scared her and threatened to detach her from reality and this beautiful moment and drag her into another part of herself, an unknown somewhere where she couldn't get back from. She felt strangely present but absent. She felt as if she was a spectator in her own life watching from another planet or another place. She tried to concentrate on Kristov's voice which was soft and low and slightly slurred at times as if he was constantly sucking a sweet. M loved his voice. It was soothing and calming.

"How is it going with your sister?" he asked, still stirring the porridge.

M was silent for a while then opened her eyes and said dreamily.

"She's falling in love with a beautiful, dark-eyed Dutch boy and having the time of her life."

Kristov nodded slowly and approvingly.

"That's great. Holland is seemingly the place for her soul."

"Seemingly," M repeated and closed her eyes again.

Kristov began to hum softly and the rice porridge bubbled. Soft snow batted the windows like flurries of albino moths.

"Oh yeah," he said, "some folklore, lets see...tomorrow, if it ever stops snowing and we can find our way to the bus stop, I'll take you to look for the *Näck*."

M sat up and leaned forward resting her chin in her hands, "What's a *Nack*?"

"The Näck, ma cherie is the Scandanavian water demon," he began grinning wickedly anticipating her curiosity.

"An evil sprite which haunts the forest's rivers and menaces travellers. He is said to have lured many unfortunate people to their deaths by drowning," Kristov continued, beginning to enjoy himself.

"Am I scaring you?" he looked at M and winked.

"No," M laughed, "but the porridge is, I think it's burnt."

"Shit! It never burns when my mother does it."

He hurriedly began stirring the burning rice and milk but it had already stuck to the bottom of the pan and was beyond rescuing.

"Never mind," M said getting up from the couch to peer into the pan. Tell me more about the Nack."

Kristov turned off the gas flame and turned to her, his intense blue eyes blazing, his mouth grinning its lopsided grin.

"Are you sure you can take it? T'is a frightening tale indeed...and we're..." he glanced, feigning nervousness, out the kitchen window at the whirling snow. "...in the woods, miles away from others, perhaps close to a Näck ourselves, who knows?"

M flopped on the couch and made a face.

"Well good luck to him, he'll be freezing his balls off out there," she began and then suddenly doubled up laughing hysterically.

"The Nack will freeze his knackers off," she managed to blurt out before emitting another spasm of raucous laughter and burying her head in the cushion.

Kristov laughed too and put his hand on his hip whilst waving the wooden porridge spoon around menacingly in the other.

"You mark my words, young M, the Näck is not to be trifled with," he went on now, feigning severity. He went over to the couch and crept up close to her, wooden spoon still in hand. He ran the other one through his fine, floppy, blond hair.

"The Näck lies in wait at the bottom of the river and often lures people in by screaming for help that he is drowning. He shrieks and moans and calls for help and it is said in tales of old, that he appears to the travellers as they come to his rescue, flailing and splashing around and disappearing under the black water. When they finally rush in to help him he grabs their legs and pulls them under until they drown." Kristov finished and flopped back on the couch.

There was silence for a moment.

"God, I scared myself," he said, hand on heart and then laughed.

Chapter 11 – *Mes Marguerites ne dorment pas ce soir*

I

It was long past midnight. Kristov had gone to bed ages ago. His mother was away for the weekend. The house was still and quiet as only houses in the countryside can be. The noise of the usual endless stream of traffic was only noticeable by its absence. The cuckoo clock in the kitchen ticked loudly. The cuckoo had long since lost the will to sing out the hour and was still. M was standing by the landing window looking out at the snowy landscape. It had stopped snowing hours ago but now the temperature had dropped below freezing and the snow lay in a thick blue-white blanket over the fields. She thought about the forest creatures lying in their chilly nests in trees and hedges. She thought about the Nack lying in wait in his icy, watery den. She shivered.

"Mes Marguerites ne dorment pas ce soir," she mumbled, her breath steaming up the window pane.

She looked like a small, lost and very sad ghost. The whiteness of her face shone against the blackness of the sleeping house. Indeed M could not sleep and had not slept for a week or more. It just would not happen any more. Her mind was too full of thoughts, images, connections and questions and now strangely, answers were coming.

Answers to the most profound and unanswerable questions life could ask. M was frightened because she believed she had discovered an amazing power. It was too big to share with anyone. She felt like she was rushing headlong into a blinding light and though she didn't want to go, she had no choice. She was exhilarated as well as terrified.

M had begun recently to be able to move things with her mind. Just by thinking about opening a desk drawer or shifting a cup along a sideboard, M had discovered that, if she concentrated long enough, she could actually do it. She had been doing it in secret since the beginning of last week and she was almost ready to tell someone about it. Maybe Kristov. But something was stopping her. Something warned her inside that maybe he would think she was crazy. Maybe he wouldn't believe her. Maybe he would laugh. Some little demon in her head told her to beware of sharing her secrets. She padded back to her room. There lay on the bedside table at least twenty sheets of A4 paper covered in manic, looped script. M found it soothing to get some of her thoughts down on paper. Then maybe she would sleep. She sat on the edge of the bed, pulled the duvet up around her and continued writing.

II

The next day, I felt much better. I could not think for the life of me why I had gotten so stirred up over this Beau character. OK, so a good looking, young guy kisses me in a bar and then we go on a date and then we end up sleeping together and then that's it, the end, finito. So what? What did I want? Him to fall in love with me? A big, heavy relationship? The happily ever after that doesn't exist anyway? Hey, I came to Amsterdam to rid myself of my old ordinary life and here I was gagging to start all over again, meet someone, settle down, nest. Have babies?

No, I didn't want that at all. I didn't want Beau either. Yes he was lovely but, no, I was not in love with him, hell I didn't even know him. Probably would have been bored to death in a month, fickle as I was. I could have kicked myself for calling him and sounding hurt and pathetic (but I *had been* hurt and pathetic), but now I could see it for what it was: a bit of fun. I rode the horse a bit too fast and I fell off but it didn't really hurt after the initial shock of hitting the ground and I had to get straight back on again. I must have been very insecure and lonely though, to have gotten so emotional over this one guy. Hell, I was becoming emotionally dependent on a person I hardly knew. This was a sure sign of instability and unhappiness. I had to make *myself* happy, not rely on some obnoxious boy barely out of his teens. I bit my lip and suddenly felt very ashamed if myself. A shame that twisted my gut and made my stomach do a loop. I had acted ridiculously because I was lonely and lost in my new life. Not because I was in love with this boy but because I craved that kind of attention from *someone* and then when they took it away, it hurt. Next time I enjoy it and take control and leave it, emotionally unattached, I thought.

I smiled to myself while I waited for the kettle to boil. I found myself suddenly thinking of Carla McClelland. I went to school with Carla McClelland. Carla McClelland wouldn't be sitting alone in an Amsterdam bed-sit with purple walls crying over some boy she hardly knew. I had been twelve, she thirteen, though to me Carla was light years ahead in maturity and sophistication. Carla McClelland always stood a few rows in front of me at school assembly each morning singing clearly and purely the school hymn, "*...we build our school on thee O Lord...*" Her uniform was neatly pressed and smelled richly of fabric softener. Her white starched collars stood pristine against her olive complexion. Her hair, straight and brown and shiny lay in a silk sheet against her head and shoulders. Mine, on the other hand was frizzy from the persistently damp weather and stuck out in all directions. It was dry and curly and unruly. How I envied Carla's shining, still crown. My skin was always red and blotchy and slightly oiled with sweat from having to rush to assembly, perpetually late. Carla was always on time, a paragon of punctuality. She was always composed, smiling and neat, like a doll in a box.

I remembered being in absolute awe of her impeccable P.E. kit. I was feeling smug for having remembered the damn thing for once, but when Carla's kit emerged from her leather-look, Adidas sports bag I was literally stunned. I at once sidestepped to hide my crumpled, creased and smelly gym things from Carla's knowing brown eyes. First came a plastic bag. 'A bag within a bag,' I thought, amazed at the concept. From the plastic bag came firstly a snow-white airtex shirt, freshly ironed and folded as if it had just been purchased from the shop. Next came an impeccably, flatly folded navy blue wrap-over gym skirt smelling of hyacinths and reminiscent of merry daisy-spotted meadows from the land of fresh laundry. I glanced shyly at my crumpled bag of crumpled kit and then in shock realised that I had forgotten my training shoes. I immediately had a mental image of them lying in a mud cake in the hall porch.

As if reading my mental image, Carla produced her pièce de résistance, her pair of shining blue and white training shoes without a mud cake in sight. Not a stone fell from the deeply grooved soles, not a grain of sand or a gravel of cat litter or a blade of dried grass. 'What dark magic is this?' I thought. And just when I thought I could not be any further amazed, Carla produced a second bag (yes two bags within a bag! A whole new wonder of P.E. kit transport technology), wherein rested a snow-virgin-white pair of woolly knee socks and a pair of dark blue knickers.

I decided that day, that I could never produce a P.E. kit like Carla McClelland. In the same way Carla could never have my frizzy hair, my mud-caked trainers or my knickers that smelled like potato bread.

When Carla left school she went to America to study Law. I pictured her now; successful, beautiful, with neat hair, perhaps married to another lawyer or a doctor or someone with an equally fine, upstanding career. She would be sitting in a sunny garden reading over her case notes whilst eating a healthy muesli breakfast and sipping decaffeinated coffee and two sunny children would be running around being delighted with everything. Carla's hair would be glossy and ethereal like a halo and her kitchen would be a paragon of sterility.

I wondered why I had adored her so much as a teenager. I felt sorry for her now and all the other Carla McClellands in the world who were scared to really live and so tried to create an impossible order of neatness, control and cleanliness. Where was the chaos Carla? The rebellious teenager? Where were the germs and the dirt and the life without a plan? I knew where I would rather be.

I wondered why I had even thought of her. Maybe I was trying to make myself feel good about being directionless, scared and out of control. I shrugged. I was spending too much time in my own head. But I liked it there.

The phone rang suddenly and my heart started to pound. I put my hand to my chest.

"Jesus!"

Why did that scare me so much? Its raucous disregard for my peace and the sanctuary of my own thoughts made me a bit cross as I leapt to pick it up.

"Hallo," I answered a bit curtly.

"It's M, *ma petite soeur*," *ma petite soeur* replied from a satellite somewhere.

"Hey great to hear from you, how is it, aren't you still in Sweden?" I asked, settling down in the corner of the sofa, my irritation forgotten all at once.

"I'm back in France, I just got back but I had to call you, I want to tell you something...something amazing... something..." There was a pause as M tried to find another word to describe the incredible thing she was about to tell me.

My heart rate went up again. "What could it be?" I thought. Had she met a boy? Fallen in love? Found a great job or won the lottery? What?

But nothing from my limited imagination could have prepared me for what I heard next.

"Charlotte," she said, her voice lowered but sounding rushed, breathless and excited and somehow scaring me to death.

"Do you believe in magic?"

My heartbeats tumbled into one another now. I caught my breath and tried to tell myself that I had misheard this strange little sentence. Strange, little and very powerful for it tore my logical and secure world away from under me and left me flailing and grabbing for something solid to hold, a foothold. Like that day in the cold Donegal sea.

I tried to gather my thoughts.

"M, have you been smoking *le hash* again?" I asked her trying to make a little joke to lighten the conversation.

The line was silent but I could hear her irritation.

At last she tutted.

"No, of course not, you...you don't understand.... I've discovered something, it's a very special secret but I've discovered it, I know about it, it's magic...and oh I'm so excited I had to tell you but I'm scared too...terrified."

'What could she have discovered that would make her think it was magic? What secret, what craziness? What had happened in Sweden to make her talk like this?'

"Had someone given her drugs, hard drugs like heroin or crack cocaine or..."

"I have to go now," she said, suddenly sounding rushed and breathless again.

"M, don't...." I began, but the click on the line told me she had hung up. M was gone. I had made her cross. I had not listened. I was not overjoyed by her secret discovery.

No. I was worried sick.

These sorts of conversations I had heard before. My grandmother suffered from manic depression nearly all of her live and in her 'high' periods would phone my mother morning, noon and night and talk non-stop rubbish in this same excited, breathless and secretive tone as if the MI5 and the CID and the secret police were all tapped in and waiting to catch her. Then she'd hang up suddenly as if she had indeed been caught and had to run off.

This call reminded me so much of these calls from granny. The content was entirely different but the pace, the tone and the unhealthy euphoria was the same. Was M having some kind of nervous breakdown? I should go there, I thought. I should take a train down there tomorrow, and if she's OK then it's fine, I'll come back.

"And if she's not?"

I took a walk out to the supermarket to clear my head and calm down. The afternoon sun was high in the sky and it was beautifully bright and sharp but the wind was cold and I had to stuff my hands in my pockets to keep them warm. Bloody May, I thought. It's so deceptive...looks beautiful from indoors then tries to flay you alive when it gets you outside!

I bought some Swedish crisp breads, some cheese, yoghurt and a small bottle of Gato Negro red. As I mulled around the shelves I decided subconsciously that I would not go to France the next day. I had to work the day after tomorrow. M was probably a bit high from some pot or something. Or over-tired from her Sweden trip. I would call her tomorrow, perhaps she'd sleep it off and we would laugh about it. I couldn't just rush off all the way to Reims on a whim. I was too easily scared. I was being oversensitive.

"If you don't know what to do, do nothing." My mother always said. Sound advice, I thought. Simple but sound. I'll sleep on it. Wait and see. See and wait.

But in this case my mother's advice was all wrong and as I walked from the supermarket back to my purple haven in a quiet suburb of Amsterdam on a windy day, two days after my 31st birthday and one day before my little sister went missing, I made the decision that was to burden me for the rest of my life. I would not go immediately to France. I would wait and see.

That night I dreamed I was back in my parent's house where we grew up. It was too small and full of furniture. M was upstairs getting ready for a Halloween party. She came down, dressed as a witch, and leapt on me. She was heavy and rough and laughing as she pinched and grabbed me. I could not get her off and I felt she was going to suffocate me.

Then the dream changed and I was walking in the pouring rain in just my socks. No shoes. Then I took off my socks as they were so wet and heavy. So I was walking in my bare feet and everywhere on the ground were sodden dog turds. Then I was suddenly eating my own sock. It was disgusting and I was trying to force it down, chewing and swallowing threads. I pulled it out of my throat and retched. But the thread was really long. I kept pulling and pulling and retching and finally on the end was a silver pendant.

I awoke feeling relief that I did not choke or suffocate.

III

Isn't it funny how we can focus on the most trivial of things as if our very lives depended on it? Getting to the supermarket before it shuts so we can get that pasta mix that will go with the leftover spinach in the fridge before it turns into a miniature swamp. Rushing to reach the post office to buy stamps to post that birthday card which will probably arrive too early in any case? Breaking our necks to catch the tram to get home in time for some crappy TV show or cycling like maniac to get home from work so we can have quality time to relax and almost getting killed in the process.

Whilst all around us near and far, earth shattering events are happening that we do or do not get to hear about. Natural disasters and unnatural ones. Death, hunger, disease, murders, rapes;

Drownings.

But when we don't have those on our doorstep to deal with, we have the trivia. The trivia becomes the live or death decision. It takes the place of dealing with the really big issues, when the really big issues are not around. And it hides them.

And isn't it funny how the fuse can be ignited far away, how the thing that is going to change your life forevermore is rushing towards you and you have *no idea* what is coming. Whilst you are blissfully perusing the supermarket aisles or quietly examining your latest lines in the bathroom mirror, the flame is eating up the fuse, running faster and gaining speed until it catches up. Then it explodes and blows you away, along with all the trivial things which seemed, an hour ago, so important and you are left blinking in shock and disbelief like a smouldering cartoon skeleton. Only the bones are left.

When I look back on the events that led to my sister's death in May 2000, I wonder (among many other things) how I could possibly not have known that she was in such danger. How could I not feel something? Of course, I was worried about her but I never for one instant thought 'M is in mortal danger'. When you live all your life with your sibling and have the deepest spiritual and mental connection, it is inconceivable that you do not sense when they are no longer alive. How can you not feel that moment, that split second when the mortal passes from this life and into the next?

I felt nothing.

IV

The next day I was sitting on a bench on the edge of the city woods near my apartment with my Dutch grammar book on my lap and feeling very at peace with the world and having one of my 'I'm damned proud of myself' moments. Yes, here I am, living abroad and it's easy, it's great, it's just like breathing. How could I ever have imagined it would be difficult and I would be unhappy and disappointed? Tsk!

It was a perfect sunny day, great 'Jesus clouds' billowed in the sky and there were camps of bluebells on the grass. It had gotten suddenly much warmer and breeze carried the promise of summer to come. The ghost of summer's future. I had tried to call M yesterday twice but just got her answer phone message in fluent French-slightly-tainted-with-Northern-Irish-accent. I left a message the second time in fluent English ever-so-slightly-touched-by-Dutch-literal-translation telling her I would 'call her soon back', hoping she would call me 'soon back' instead and that I was sorry I had been a bit short with her last time. I guessed she was busy as usual or maybe slightly pissed at me for not indulging her in her new magical discovery.

V

M was on the Paris train heading back to Reims. She was a bit late with it but she hadn't forgotten Charlotte's birthday card. She'd carefully cut a Leffe six pack box and Made a pretty birthday card and written upon the back;

"The cutest thing is, you don't even know that you are so funny and such a real character, cos you're so 'je m'en foutiste'... cos like me no one ever told you it before and you need a kick up the fesses of positive abruptness.

Just cos you appreciate the family of friendship and the trivia and creativity of life...you're a fellow culture slag, a closet linguistic fuck-up with no shame. with the gift of the blah and supa of the Micks...the lebenlust and rough and readiness of the Krauts..the bon goût of the Grooda but also their sloppiness...

So just learn a little largom and you can blah the rest!

Fear not! You won't frighten off these anges souffrants like the Karringar al al Suedoise...cos, coupled with your elfin beauty and the shining smile of the North, you're a star...and the Kramm that you need, I know where that comes from!'

M wrote furiously whilst riding on the train. She was focusing hard on anything she could to try to take her mind off what she had just seen. She had maybe been asleep in the train carriage. It was one of those old fashioned trains with closed in carriages seating six people. It was early in the morning and she was alone, surrounded by gently rocking metal and glass. Maybe she had dreamed it.

For suddenly, just outside the sliding door she saw a women walking towards her with her hands outstretched. Her face was a contorted grimace of agony, for her whole body was on fire. No sound emitted from this violent and fantastic apparition. The agony silenced the scream. The hands were blackening. The fire was consuming the head. The hair melting to fibreglass. The woman banged on the window and M jumped against the side of the carriage, her brain in absolute panic, her heart trying to escape its cage of ribs.

Then she was gone. M was sure she'd been awake. That was no nightmare. Or if it was a nightmare it had somehow broken through into her reality. Wasn't that called a hallucination?

M tried to deep breath to calm herself. Her heartbeat began at last to slow into an acceptable rhythm. With trembling hands she picked up Charlotte's birthday card again and tried to reread it. She noticed her hands were damp with perspiration and she wiped them on her jeans then stared down in disbelief as a marvellous horror washed over her like a cold bath.

Her hands were charcoal black.

M got off the train at Reims station, so familiar to her now but also today, so odd. People were looking at her. Why would she care, let them, the fuck, look!

But today was different. M could see their ugly faces close up, their nasal hairs, their moles and warts, their snarling yellow teeth. My God, she thought, they look like wolves. Two black youths walked by and laughed. She could hear their snickers rasping in her head but not in her ears. Their faces were dark like silken ebony, their teeth too white.

Their teeth hurt her eyes. She shied away from them and bumped into a small toad-like man with a large orange shopping bag. On the side of the shopping bag was a smiling pink pig advertising pork.

'I don't think a pig would advertise pork,' M thought.

The pig winked at her. M put her head down and walked very fast back to her flat trying as much as possible not to see anything on the way.

Her head was buzzing as if many bees had entered it and couldn't find their way out.

She ran upstairs to her little musty green flat and slammed the door shut.

'Now, I'm safe,' she thought, and sighed all the bees out.

M went to the bathroom to let cold water run over her hands and to try to wash away some of the horror of the journey as well as the charcoal. She looked in the mirror and emitted a short sharp sound, a yelp like a small animal in desperate pain.

Her face was black with soot too.

Chapter 12 – *Mes Marguerites dorment bien ce soir*

I – Thursday

After the weekend, I was back to working shifts. I didn't mind too much. At least I didn't have to worry about spending each evening completely alone. I still hadn't had a call from M and was now really worried. Maybe I should have gone there on my days off, but I had an appointment with an employment agency dealing with international organisations and I was eager to get a job away from this hospital. I wanted a desk job and my weekends and evening free. But maybe something was really wrong. Why didn't M call me? But still my rational side told me to wait and be still. It was only just over a week since I'd heard from her. It wasn't the first time but oh, that strange call. I trudged through the rest of the day, heavy in heart and sick in the stomach and finally at 4.45 p.m. the end of my shift came. I was released from the hospital, disinfected stink into the warm, bright, billowing Amsterdam air and cycled speedily homeward.

As I opened the door, I immediately went to the phone and dialled my voice mail. "*U heeft negen nieuwe berichten,*" the automated Dutch robot lady said.

"M!" I thought feeling relief, joy and then anger that she'd made me so worried.

But there were no messages. I had nine missed calls. And no number recorded to return them. Nine missed calls? Who on earth was calling me nine times in one day? I'd never had nine missed calls in my life. What the hell was so urgent? Why wasn't there a message then? A number to return the call? I felt sick to the stomach.

I sat down. Suddenly my legs were shaky and buckling under my weight. Something was terribly wrong here. Something awful was happening or had happened. M was in trouble. I instinctively knew these calls were either from her or relating to her recent silence. Now I was gnawing my knuckles with worry. Who could I call? What should I do? Call the police (and tell them what exactly?) Should I call home? Yes, great idea and worry the hell out of dad.

No, I had to think it through. I stayed calm and went to the kitchenette to make some tea. This is what the Irish always do in a crisis. Make a nice cup of tea. The familiar ritual of filling the kettle, getting a teaspoon from the rickety drawer and taking a tea bag from the box already began to soothe my frayed nerves a bit. I poured the hot water into the cup and tears pricked the back of my eyes as I read the lettering on the side, white on blue. It said *Leipziger Weinachtsmarkt*. One of M's souvenirs from the Christmas market in Leipzig, Germany. 'Where was she?' I breathed into the cup of water and let the steam moisten and soothe my eyelids. Maybe I had a wrong number? But nine times?

The phone sounded abruptly like a klaxon from another world and I almost dropped my cup.

It was Taru. She sounded worried and my knees gave way again as I melted into the couch a second time as I listened to her halting, slow English asking if I had seen M or if I knew where she might be. I managed to make a sound which she interpreted in the negative and then she told me that she and Angéline, (little sweet, dark, French Angéline), had not seen M since she got back from Sweden. She had not been to the university, nor showed up for lessons, nor called anyone. And finally last night in desperation, the two had gone to the back of M's apartment block and climbed up to her back window sill, (where the desiccated cactus lived), prized it open and entered the room to find the front door wide open and M's absence burning a hole in the dark, green room.

"Don't worry, don't worry" She reassured me. We are looking for her...maybe she just stayed in Sweden or something. Do you have the number of this...this Kristov in Sweden?"

"I think so, somewhere," my voice sounded far away to me. I was talking to myself from somewhere in the future or from the past, from the womb.

"We will call police," she said quietly and then added to warm me, though it chilled me to the bone.

"And when we find her, we'll kill her."

II – Saturday

"She's already dead," Beau's voice whispered in my ear as we lay like spoons on his bed watching his red, crystal fairy lights, blinking at us.

I woke up with a start and my heartbeats kicked into warp speed. I put my hand to my chest as if to keep them inside and slowly began plucking fragments of the day's events from the tired neurons in my brain. Some lights were on. Some lights were off. Some were disconnected entirely. M was missing. Taru had called me. I had a dream about Beau. A nightmare. That's all. Nothing bad had happened. I threw my head back onto my pillow. What was that idiot doing now in my dream?

I switched on the bedside light, then the main light. I walked into the kitchenette and switched that light on too. I opened the kitchen window and breathed deeply. The air outside smelled like frozen cream.

It was 5 a.m. The hour of the sleepless and the wretched. It was too early to call Taru. Too early to go outside and lose myself in the day. Too early to call Kristov. Too early to call my father. In fact I was putting all these things off. At least now there was nothing to know. It could go either way from here. M could turn up somewhere. She had gone missing before and sailed back into our lives without a care. She had once taken an impromptu motorbike ride for the weekend with an ex boyfriend and just forgot to tell anyone where she was going. It was probably fine and we were all worried for nothing. Taru would be embarrassed that she'd troubled the police. I wouldn't call my father yet. I didn't want to worry him unnecessarily. It was after all only seven days since I'd heard from M. It wasn't the first time that two or three weeks had even lapsed without a phone call. But this felt different. Yes, I would call Kristov just to make sure she hadn't gone back to Sweden.

But one thing haunted the rest of my shallow sleep that night. M had gone out in an awful hurry if she left her apartment door wide open.

III – Sunday

Kristov called me back after I had left several messages on his voicemail. No he hadn't seen M since she left Sweden on May 2nd. She'd been fine, 'seemingly' had a great holiday and he hoped she'd show up soon. I asked if she'd seemed 'herself' or if he'd observed any odd behaviour. He paused for quite a long time then laughed and answered 'no more than usual.'

I said I'd let him know when she showed up.

Taru called. On Saturday they had brought M's photograph to the police and posted some pictures of her around Reims. Someone said they saw a girl answering to her description walking along M's street towards the station carrying a rucksack on Friday 5th May. No, there was no need for me to come to Reims. They were already doing everything.

Taru called again. M's bag had been found in a bar, Le Castel Roc. It had been there since Friday. The barman saw she'd left it behind and took it behind the bar. He didn't know how to contact her and reckoned she'd come back soon enough to get it. Everything was there. Her purse, money, credit cards, cheque book, house keys, camera and some other things;

Candles

Incense

Cloves of garlic

Photos of our mother (who died in 1999)

A leaflet called, *The Devil's Bible* in Swedish and English

The Little book of calm, in French.

I remembered a snippet of a conversation we'd had in a supermarket in Amsterdam once, a million years ago. M's shopping list had read: white spirits (for painting), candles and *lucifers*. She had written the word for matches in Dutch as we both thought it was funny and strange to call matches lucifers.

"Are you going to have a séance then M?" I had asked and we both doubled up with laughter.

My stomach tensed. Where could M be without money? I pictured her wandering the fields of the Northern French

Champagne region, a scarecrow figure, no money, no food, lost, sick and frightened. I couldn't bear it.

Taru called again. Apparently she had just heard that two colleagues of M's had called by last Thursday evening as she hadn't showed up at work all week. Susie and Raymond. Two other language assistants were worried and dropped by to check on her. She had been manic and talking non stop and Susie had offered to stay the night with her and take her to a doctor the next day if she wasn't feeling better. M had said she had never felt better but promised to stay home and see a doctor soon. She had rushed them out and slammed the door shut.

IV – Friday

M was walking by the canal. It was late in the evening but it was still quite light. She crossed the bridge away from the city side and towards the old abandoned cottage with the overgrown tangled garden. The sky was tender pink in the light of early dusk. The promise of sleep, stillness and peace hung in the mild air. M was happy, oh so happy. She had given up all her worldly goods, her possessions, her flat, her money. She had discovered the true secret of life. In essence life is just one bodily form of the deepest spirituality. It all made so much sense now. The image on the train of the burning woman. That was she, M, before she learned to give up her material possessions, her friends, her physical being. They were meaningless. It was only she now, her soul and her essence with nature that mattered. That was the secret, the magic of it all and she could do anything now. There were no restrictions of physics, science or society. No boundaries. Just an infinite imagination and a spirit that could go anywhere and be anything. Immortality.

She had been burning before, burning with unfulfilled passion and worries. The fire was fuelled with material possessions and ignited by relationships. Now the fire was out. She was becoming cool. Like the water.

She sat by the canal in her garden of golden apples.

When she was a child M had made up a story about the garden of golden apples. She believed that in many years (ten or so seemed a safe enough length of time as to be infinite when one is a child) that the world would cease to function in its present civilised form and that food and water would become scarce. People would begin to die from hunger and disease but not she, not us, not we who knew about the garden of golden apples. Therein lay food in abundance, fruits and vegetables growing on trees and bushes ripe for the picking and delicious, juicy, sweet golden- coloured apples begging to be eaten. But it would only be for the chosen few who knew the secret.

Finally now M was in her garden, by the canal. Detach from the material and physical world and you can be anything you want to be. Ride unicorns all day and gaze all night at the stars in the garden of golden apples.

It was perfect but first she had to cool off even more. To make sure all the fires were out. All that burning had to be stopped for good.

It was almost dark now. The water on the canal was black like a pool of ink, cool ink, deliciously soothing. M stood up and walked quietly to the edge. She was smiling, relieved and happy she had finally come to this decision to pass from fire and into water.

She walked, still smiling, into the water.

V– Monday

"Are you alone?" came the urgent voice of Susie Jordan, M's colleague, her lilting Liverpool accent shot with emotion.

I was alone, as usual. I froze at the sound of her voice and felt like I was going to vomit. This was it. Something bad. The word bad in my head sounded so inadequate.

I whispered a "Yes, but it's OK."

Tell me Susie, I thought, Carry on. Get it over with. I am already on the edge of the abyss. It will be a relief to just let myself fall in.

She went on calmly and I could hear it in her voice, desperately trying not to cry.

"They found a body, Charlotte... and it's M. I saw her today. It's her. I'm so sorry, I wouldn't call you if I wasn't sure."

"Where?" I whispered.

"In the river Marne, about nine kilometres from Reims, near Champigny, if you know it, if it makes any difference," Susie carried on.

"It appears she drowned there, some days ago in fact, probably on the fourth or fifth."

And now I am falling in. The abyss is welcoming me. All that blackness blanking out everything, every emotion, every sense, thought, feeling.

"Thanks Susie" I said, "Thank you for doing that...." and then added because it was the plain truth, "now I don't have to."

VI

The next few days passed by but I have no real recollection of them. I went to France where I stayed with Susie. I cried with Taru and Angéline and even Guy. The police interviewed me and everything I said was interpreted (badly). I had blood samples and cheek cell samples taken to identify my DNA. I arranged a coffin and repatriation. I called my dad, my friends in Belfast. M's friends from all over the world were calling me and asking me what the hell had happened. I didn't really know what to tell them.

The whole world was in shock. My world at least. A great white, atom bomb mushroom shock. The heat from it made my eyes water. It melted my reason and gladly it numbed my emotions. M had managed to shock us all again. This time she really blasted us. This time we would never recover.

And yet the sun still rose and set. The world still spun on its axis and the universe expanded infinitely and we still laughed sometimes.

A few days later the police gave me back her bag which had previously been behind the bar at the Castel Roc. Amongst the obvious contents and a few more sinister additions like the candles, incense and garlic and, lying at the bottom, completely discarded, broken and dust covered, was the unicorn, our talisman. Our glittering, scintillating, iridescent, mythical creature of glass. Its iridescence now dulled by grease and dust. One of its front legs was missing. M had had him in her bag all this time and yet thought she'd lost him. Or had she known all along?

I sat for some time on the floor of Susie's flat nursing the broken unicorn and remembering the day we found him and then just remembering.

Finding the unicorn again made me think of the human necessity to be always looking for something, searching and at times going on long journeys both in the physical sense and the psychological and yet the thing we are really searching for is usually right by us all the time. We just don't see it. Like Dorothy's journey to the Emerald city in that grand old classic *The Wizard of Oz*. She had to travel over the rainbow to find out, after all, that there was no place like home.

Perhaps I should go home now too.

VII

We were sitting on the terrace of a café in the Dutch city of Delft. It was a sharp, cold, windy spring day and the wind whipped M's stringy strawberry blond locks onto her screwed up face. She wore no sunglasses and squinted into the strong sunlight whilst the ash from her home made cigarette blew around her. A half drunk, now cold cup of coffee sat in front of her. The collar of her black, retro leather jacket was turned up against the cold. Her knuckles were red. Her lips were chapped but smiling.

I was utterly confused. To all intent and purpose this was a happy, comfortable afternoon coffee with my sister but something was dreadfully wrong inside of me. But I just couldn't put my finger on it. I struggled to piece it together like trying to remember the fragments of an important dream but not quite reaching it. It floated away form me in the wind. I tried smile but it twisted my gut. Oh there was something so wrong with this picture. Why couldn't I just relax and enjoy it? Why wasn't I relieved? Why should I be relieved? M cocked her head and screwed up her eyes even tighter. She raised one eyebrow quizzically at me as if she had asked me a question and was now waiting expectantly for an answer.

Then suddenly, I remembered. I had it in my grasp. I suddenly knew why it felt so wrong but so good at the same time.

M was dead. She died a year ago and here I was sitting in a café with her, just like old times. I frantically tried to apply a logical explanation to the scene.

I leapt out of my chair.

"M, how can you be here,…….. there…I mean right in front of me, talking, smoking? You, you're dead," I blurted out hearing my voice inside my head as if spoken from a deep cavern. It travelled upwards from my core in slow motion. It was blurred and furred and it choked me. She cocked her head even further and grinned even wider and then began to laugh. Then she too stood up, reached first for her tobacco, then her bag and slung it over her shoulder. Then she looked me in the eyes and stopped smiling. She gave me the briefest hint of a wink before turning and walking away.

"I know," she said.